喚醒你的英文語感！

Get a Feel for English !

喚醒你的英文語感！

Get a Feel for English!

This is a book **for you** to...

勇闖陌生國度＋打理食衣住行＋建立人際網絡＋深入他國文化

Campus life

Campus Life

留學英文 很有聊

主題式進階會話，有志氣自然越聊越起勁！

總編審：王復國
作　者：Lily Yang（楊智媛）

破除留學生活的語言難關，
培養用英文「生活」的能力！
課堂上學得豐碩，
在國外活得精彩！
打開溝通之門，
豐富知識之旅！

Start

N

貝塔語言出版
Beta Multimedia Publishing

附 2 片生存 CD

序

In May of 2002, after four years in Charlottesville, Virginia, I finally had "the honor of honors" and graduated from the University of Virginia (UVA). Time had flown by, and while I was sad to see the end of my university career, I realized that it had forever shaped and altered me for the future.

Being an international student is not an easy thing. You have to leave your friends and family, and study in a foreign and sometimes strange environment. You'll encounter communication problems, cultural misunderstandings, and homesickness. Looking at my complete mess of a room the day after I moved in, I realized that this was the time I was truly on my own. I didn't have my family to rely on. I didn't have my mother to help me with my laundry! I was able to get through these difficulties with the help of my international host — an older student who helped me settle in. I became an international host myself, and helped younger international students deal with any problems they encountered. I was able to pass along my knowledge, experience, and advice, and that is what I also hope to do with this book.

This book is full of information to help you tackle the challenge of studying abroad. In it, you'll find everything you need, be it tackling housing issues, opening up a bank account, sorting out transportation, or even just having fun and mixing drinks with your friends! Remember that this opportunity usually only happens once. Cherish it, make the most of your time there, and have fun!

Lily Y S

在 2002 年 5 月，在維吉尼亞州的夏洛特維爾市生活了四年之後，我總算以「榮譽學生」的身份從維吉尼亞大學畢業了。時光飛逝，雖然感傷於見到大學生涯就此結束，但我瞭解大學時的一切已永久塑造和改變了我，未來再也不一樣了。

當外籍學生並非易事，你得離開朋友和家人到國外唸書，有時環境還非常陌生。你會遇到溝通問題、文化上的誤解以及想家。回顧我剛遷入那天，把房間搞得一團混亂的情況，我知道這次我真的一切都得靠自己了。沒有家人可以依賴，也沒有媽媽可以幫我處理髒衣服了！所幸有國際招待員（一名幫我熟悉環境、年紀稍長的學生）的幫忙，我才能夠解決這些難題。後來我自己也當了國際招待員，幫助年紀較小的外籍學生應付任何遇到的問題，我得以把我得到的知識、經驗和建議傳遞出去，而這也是我透過這本書希望達到的目的。

本書充滿了各種資訊，可幫助你應付留學時遇到的挑戰。在本書裡，你需要的資訊應有盡有，可用它來應付住的問題、開立銀行帳戶、挑選交通工具，甚或是和朋友玩樂，享受調酒的樂趣！記住，留學往往是一生僅此一次的機會。好好把握，盡量豐富經驗，享受其中的樂趣！

楊智媛

CONTENTS

每所學校都會舉辦新生訓練，幫助學生熟悉環境。新生訓練可能需要一天的時間，但有時也會長達一星期，通常外籍學生都有自己新生訓練的預訂日程，討論所有外籍學生都必須面對的一些特定議題。

大部分的學校規定一年級生要住宿，如此一來新生就有機會認識朋友，很快地熟悉環境。每所學校的宿舍不同，但都傾向遵循一個基本概念：二人住一寢，共用一間浴室和其他房間。

如果你是住學校宿舍，搬家很簡單。但如果是在外自己租公寓，就稍微麻煩一點了。你得自己搞定水電瓦斯、電話線、網路線，也可能得自行購買家具，以及其他任何遷入新居所需的物品，好讓新公寓有家的感覺。

出國後馬上要辦的一件事就是開立銀行帳戶。最好選一家分行多的銀行，這樣找提款機時會比較方便。開戶時，有的銀行會要求你提供社會安全號碼，不過規模較大的銀行，只要求外籍人士提供護照就可以開戶。可以先攜帶一點現金和旅行支票開戶，之後再把錢匯進帳戶裡。

CONTENTS

人物介紹

　　我叫 Annie，今年 18 歲，從小在台北長大。我和你一樣，唸英文好幾年了。但和你不同的是，我的英文能力有機會更加往上提升，因為我申請到美國的一所大學，終於可以到英文環境中學英文和許多其他東西。我對商業和媒體有興趣，也準備在畢業後留在美國工作一年。我即將和室友同住，有一點緊張，但這可是和當地學生交朋友的最佳管道。總而言之，我得打包了。記住，你也可以擁有與我相同的經驗！

　　我是 Kevin，來自高雄。我 26 歲，大學時主修工程，現在出國唸電機研究所。我的學校讓我在系上當助教，對我的經濟狀況不無小補。有時候我覺得帶研討課很難，但是我可以真正地學會用英文溝通；我也認識了很多朋友，因為我的研究所中外籍學生很多。等拿到學位，我會進一家在亞洲有很多分公司的工程事務所工作。我最喜歡的一句話就是：我一定可以的！

Chapter 1

Orientation 新生訓練

Orienting yourself

Every school holds an orientation to help students get settled in. Orientation may last a day, or even a week, and all the events may seem quite overwhelming at first. While you may be preoccupied with moving in and setting up your room, orientation serves a very important purpose. Meetings and events are scheduled to prepare you for your life at the school. While some events require attendance and others don't, international students usually have their own orientation schedule, containing specifically chosen topics that all international students must address.

熟悉環境

每所學校都會舉辦新生訓練,幫助學生熟悉新環境。新生訓練可能會持續一整天,或甚至一星期,而且剛開始的時候,一大堆的活動可能會令人吃不消。雖然你可能忙著搬家和安頓住處,但新生訓練還是有其重要的功能。集會和活動的安排都是要幫助你適應校園生活。雖然有的活動一定得參加,有的不一定,但通常外籍學生都有自己新生訓練的預訂日程,包括討論所有外籍學生都必須面對的一些特定議題。

Top 10 必會字彙

CD **1-02**

★ **information session**
[ˌɪnfə`meʃən ˌsɛʃən]

n. 說明會

★ **major requirement**
[`medʒɚ rɪ`kwaɪrmənt]

n. 主要必修科目

★ **pre-requisite**
[pri`rɛkwəzɪt]

n. 前題；先決條件（＝ pre-req）

★ **course catalog**
[`kors `kætḷˌɔg]

n. 課程目錄
（或即 general catalog）

★ **register**
[`rɛdʒɪstɚ]

v. 註冊

★ **registrar's office**
[`rɛdʒɪˌstrɑrz `ɔfɪs]

n. 註冊組

★ **eligible**
[`ɛlɪdʒəbḷ]

adj. 符合資格的

★ **grant**
[grænt]

n. 獎學金；助學金

★ **work-study**
[`wɝk`stʌdɪ]

n. 校內的工作機會

★ **permanent address**
[`pɝmənənt ə`drɛs]

n. 永久住址

CD 1-03

1 A: Are you going to that department information session this afternoon?

　 B: Of course. They will be discussing some changes to the major requirements.

　 A: 你今天下午會去參加那場系所說明會嗎？

　 B: 當然。他們會討論一些針對主要必修科目所做的改變。

---

2 A: I wonder if there are any pre-reqs for this course.

　 B: Just check the course catalog. All that information is in there.

　 A: 不知道修這門課有沒有什麼先決條件？

　 B: 看一下課程目錄吧。所有的相關資訊都在裡面。

---

3 A: We can register for classes online before the 28th.

　 B: I know. After that, you need to do it in person at the registrar's office.

　 A: 我們 28 號以前可以上網選課。

　 B: 我知道。之後你就得自己親自到註冊組選課了。

---

4 A: Am I eligible for any grants or work-study?

　 B: I'll check. Let me have your name and permanent address.

　 A: 我的資格符不符合申請獎學金或校內的工作機會？

　 B: 我查一下。請告訴我你的名字和永久住址。

你可以跟我這樣說

CD **1-04**

Dialogue A

Annie meets with her academic advisor to finalize her class schedule.

Annie: Hello Professor Roy. My name is Annie Wang.

Prof. Roy: Yes. You're one of my freshmen advisees. Sit down and let's go through your schedule.

Annie: Here are the classes I've already chosen. *(Annie hands him her course card.)*

Prof. Roy: I see you've signed up for Psych 101, Statistics 120, Writing 102, and Biology 131. No foreign language?

Annie: I'm exempt from the foreign language requirement because English is my second language.

Prof. Roy: What do you plan to major in?

Annie: I think I'll do business. But I'm also interested in media.

Prof. Roy: Why don't you take a media class? You only have twelve credits so far. Most students average fifteen each semester.

Annie: I'd like to, but they're all full.

Prof. Roy: You can wait and see if anyone will drop out of the class, or you can e-mail the professor and be put on a waiting list. Many students change their classes after the first week anyway. I think you're in good shape. Any questions?

Annie: No. I think I'll just take another look at the schedule of classes and decide on a media class.

Prof. Roy: All right. If you have any other questions, you can e-mail me, or feel free to drop by during my office hours. They're posted on the door.

Annie: Great, thanks for your help!

安妮與她的課業指導教授見面以確定課表。

安妮： 洛依教授，您好。我叫安妮·王。

洛依教授：是的，妳是我的一年級輔導生。請坐，我們來看一看妳的課表。

安妮： 這些是我已經選好的課程。（*安妮將課表交給他。*）

洛依教授：看來妳已經選了心理學 101、統計學 120、寫作課 102 跟生物學 131。沒有選外語課嗎？

安妮： 我可以免修必修的外語課，因為英文是我的第二語言。

洛依教授：妳準備主修什麼呢？

安妮： 我想主修商學，但對媒體傳播也有興趣。

洛依教授：妳何不選修一門傳播課？目前為止妳只修了 12 個學分，大部分的學生每學期平均修 15 個學分。

安妮： 我很想，但是每堂課都額滿了。

洛依教授：妳可以等一等，看看有沒有人退選，不然可以寫電子郵件給教授，在候補名單上登記。反正很多學生在第一個星期後會改修其他課程。我覺得妳狀況不錯。還有什麼問題嗎？

安妮： 沒有了。我想我會看一下課表，然後決定是不是要修一門傳播課。

洛依教授：好的。如果有任何其他問題，可以寫電子郵件給我，或者在我的辦公時間來找我。我的辦公時間就公佈在門上。

安妮： 太好了，謝謝您的協助！

[Words & Phrases]

· advisor [əd`vaɪzɚ] *n.* 指導教授

· advisee [əd,vaɪ`zi] *n.* 受選課指導的學生

· sign up 報名參加

· exempt [ɪg`zɛmpt] *adj.* 免除……義務的

· credit [`krɛdɪt] *n.* 學分

· drop [drɑp] *v.* 退選

· waiting list [`wetɪŋ ,lɪst] *n.* 候補名單

· office hours [`ɔfɪs ,aurz] *n.* 辦公時間

你可以跟我這樣說

CD **1-05**

Dialogue B

Kevin goes to the Financial Aid office to fill out paperwork for his teaching assistant position.

Kevin: Hi, I'm a new graduate student. I'll be a teaching assistant for Professor Rody and I was told to come in and fill out some payroll forms.

Secretary: Which department is Professor Rody in? And I'll need to see your passport and I-20.

Kevin: OK. Here you go. *(He hands the stuff to the secretary.)* She's in the Engineering school. I was wondering how I'll get paid.

Secretary: You'll be mailed a check on the 1st and 15th of every month. Taxes will automatically be deducted.

Kevin: Am I allowed to have more than one job?

Secretary: Only in the university. Your visa restricts you to on-campus employment. But it looks like you'll be working at least ten hours a week for Professor Rody. You probably won't have time for another job.

Kevin: If I T.A. for another department, will I need to come in and sign these forms again?

Secretary: No. The new department will take care of the transfer for you. All right, please sign here. *(She points to the bottom of a form.)*

Kevin: I still have to pay for the remainder of my tuition fees. I was wondering where the Bursar's office is.

Secretary: It's just downstairs. You'll want to pay your tuition as soon as possible; otherwise, you won't be able to register for classes.

Kevin: That's what my advisor said! Thanks for your help.

凱文到助學辦公室填寫當助教所需的表格。

凱文：妳好，我是新來的研究生。我將會是羅迪教授的助教，我被告知要到這裡填寫一些薪資表格。

秘書：羅迪教授是哪一系的？我得看一下你的護照和 I-20。

凱文：好，在這裡。*（他把證件交給秘書。）*她是工程學院的教授。我想知道我的薪水會如何支付。

秘書：你會在每個月的 1 號和 15 號收到一張支票，稅會自動從中扣除。

凱文：我可以有一個以上的工作嗎？

秘書：只能在學校裡面。你的簽證限制你只能在校內工作。不過看來你每週會幫羅迪教授工作至少十小時，大概也沒時間做其他工作了。

凱文：如果到其他的系當助教，我是不是也得回來重新填寫這些表格？

秘書：不需要。新的系會幫你處理移轉事宜。好了，請在這裡簽名。*（指著表格下方。）*

凱文：我還必須繳剩餘的學費。不知道出納室在哪裡？

秘書：就在樓下。你最好儘快繳學費，否則沒辦法選課。

凱文：我的輔導教授也是這麼說的！謝謝妳的幫忙。

[Words & Phrases]

- Financial Aid office [faɪˋnænʃəl ˋed ͵ɔfɪs] *n.* 助學辦公室
- teaching assistant [ˋtitʃɪŋ əͺsɪstənt] *n.* 助教 (=T.A.)
- payroll [ˋpeͺrol] *n.* 受薪人員名單
- I-20 為美國學校提供自費留學生申請簽證時的入學證明文件
- deduct [dɪˋdʌkt] *v.* 扣除
- restrict [rɪˋstrɪkt] *v.* 限制
- on-campus [ˋɑn͵kæmpəs] *adj.* 校內的
- tuition [tuˋɪʃən] *n.* 學費
- Bursar's office [ˋbɝsɚz ˋɔfɪs] *n.* 出納室

留學　超實用單字

CD **1-06**

Orienting Yourself to Your School 認識校園

★ social [ˋsoʃəl] *n.* 聯誼會

You: Are you going to the ice-cream social in the Student Center?
Friend: Sure. It'll be a great way to meet other freshmen.

你： 你會去學生中心的冰淇淋聯誼會嗎？
朋友： 當然，這是認識其他大一生很好的管道。

★ add / drop form [ˋæd / ˋdrɑp ˏfɔrm] *n.* 加選／退選單

You: I really hate my calculus[1] class, but it's already past the drop deadline.
Friend: Just withdraw[2] from the class. Fill out an add/drop form at the registrar's office.

你： 我真的很討厭我的微積分課，但是退選期限已經過了。
朋友： 取消這門課就好了。到註冊組填寫一張加退選單。

★ [3] lecture [ˋlɛktʃɚ] *n.* 講課

Friend: Professor Madison's lecture is always really interesting.
You: No wonder his class is completely full.

朋友： 麥迪森教授上課都非常地有趣。
你： 難怪他的課都爆滿。

[Word List]

1. calculus [ˋkælkjələs] *n.* 微積分
2. withdraw [wɪðˋdrɔ] *v.* 取消；撤回

★ discussion class [dɪ`skʌʃən ˏklæs] *n.* 討論會

You: Are you going to take History 420?
Friend: I'd like to, but it requires a discussion class and they're all in the early morning!

你：   你會選修歷史 420 嗎？
朋友：   我想啊，但是規定得參加討論會，而討論會都排在一大早！

★ seminar [`sɛməˏnar] *n.* 研討課

Professor: You should take my Politics, Sociology[1] and History seminar. It's a small class and you'll have a chance to really discuss your thoughts and ideas.
You: I'd like to, but I'm already signed up for fifteen credits.

教授：   你應該選我的政治、社會與歷史專題研討課。這堂課採小班制，你會有機會討論你的想法和意見。
你：   我很想，但我已經修了 15 個學分了。

Financial Issues 經濟問題

★ scholarship [`skɑləˏʃɪp] *n.* 獎學金

Professor: I've just nominated[2] you for the Wilson scholarship. If you win it, your tuition fees for next semester will be taken care of.
You: Really? That's wonderful. It would take a bit of the financial burden off of my parents.

教授：   我剛提名你申請威爾森獎學金。如果獲獎，你下個學期的學費就沒問題了。
你：   真的嗎？那太好了。這樣就可以幫我父母減輕一點經濟負擔。

[Word List]

1. sociology [ˏsoʃɪˋɑlədʒɪ] *n.* 社會學   2. nominate [`nɑməˏnet] *v.* 提名

CD **1-07**

⭐ minimum wage [ˋmɪnəməm ˋwedʒ] *n.* 最低工資

You: How much does a job at the library pay?

Friend: I'm not sure. But all university jobs pay at least minimum wage.

你： 在圖書館工作的薪水是多少？

朋友： 我不確定，不過大學內所有的工作都至少會支付最低工資。

⭐ hourly wage [ˋaurlɪ ˋwedʒ] *n.* 時薪

Friend: Do you get a salary or are you paid by the hour?

You: I have an hourly wage.

朋友： 你拿的是月薪還是按小時計酬？

你： 我拿的是時薪。

⭐ local address [ˋlokļ əˋdrɛs] *n.* 當地住址

You: The school sent my bookstore bill to my parents by mistake.

Roommate: Make sure the school knows your local address. Get it changed at the registrar's office.

你： 學校錯把我書店的帳單寄給我爸媽了。

室友： 你得確定學校有你當地的住址。到註冊組去改吧。

☆ timesheet [ˈtaɪmˌʃit] *n.* 工作時間記錄卡

You: Why are you in such a hurry?

Friend: I can't be late for work because my boss checks the timesheet everyday.

你：   你為什麼這麼趕？

朋友：   我上班不能遲到，因為我老闆每天都會查工作時間記錄卡。

☆ payment plan [ˈpemənt ˌplæn] *n.* 分期付款

You: Our tuition fees are so high.

Roommate: Yeah. That's why I opted[1] for the payment plan. That way I don't have to pay it all at once.

你：   我們的學費好貴。

室友：   是啊，所以我才會選擇分期付款。這麼一來，就不需要一次全部付清。

[Word List]

1. opt [ɑpt] *v.* 選擇

Fall Orientation Schedule

Day One:

 9:00 a.m. Check-In at Student Center and get Student I.D. pictures taken

11:00 a.m. Meet Your Orientation Leaders in Avery Auditorium[1]

12:00 p.m. Lunch in Main Hall Dining Room

 2:00 p.m. School Advising Meetings & Course Scheduling Workshop

 4:15 p.m. Joining the Community in the Main Ballroom

 5:00 p.m. Student Life Issues in the Main Ballroom
Have your questions about student life at the university answered by a panel of students.

 6:15 p.m. Dinner in Main Hall Dining Room

 7:45 p.m. Evening Activities at the Fitness Center

10:00 p.m. Small Group Meeting with Orientation Leaders in Dorms

Day Two:

 8:00 a.m. Continental[2] Breakfast in Baylor Dining Hall

 9:00 a.m. Course Schedule Advising at Individual Faculty[3] Offices

10:00 a.m. Tours of Buildings *(meet on steps of Main Hall every hour)*

11:30 a.m. Lunch in Main Hall Dining Room

 2:00 p.m. Tour of Harrison and Wylder Libraries — Harrison Library Lobby

 3:00 p.m. International Student Orientation in Morrison 131

 6:15 p.m. Dinner in Main Hall Dining Room

 8:00 p.m. Ice-cream social in First Year Dorms Quad[4]

10:00 p.m. Last meeting with Orientation Leaders

[翻　譯]

秋季學期新生訓練日程表

第一天：

9:00 a.m. 到學生中心辦理登記，拍攝學生證照片

11:00 a.m. 到艾夫利禮堂認識你的新生訓練小隊長

12:00 p.m. 午餐，主廳餐廳

2:00 p.m. 學校輔導會議與課程安排工作坊

4:15 p.m. 融入社群，主舞廳

5:00 p.m. 與學生生活相關之議題，主舞廳

由學生小組回答與大學生活相關的問題。

6:15 p.m. 晚餐，主廳餐廳

7:45 p.m. 晚間活動，健身中心

10:00 p.m. 與新生訓練小隊長舉行小組會議，宿舍

第二天：

8:00 a.m. 歐陸早餐，貝樂餐廳

9:00 a.m. 課程建議，個別職員辦公室

10:00 a.m. 參觀學校大樓 *（每小時於主廳的階梯上集合）*

11:30 a.m. 午餐，主廳餐廳

2:00 p.m. 參觀哈里森圖書館和威爾得圖書館——哈里森圖書館大廳

3:00 p.m. 外籍學生新生訓練，莫理森 131 室

6:15 p.m. 晚餐，主廳餐廳

8:00 p.m. 冰淇淋聯誼會，一年級生宿舍的四方院

10:00 p.m. 與新生訓練小隊長開最後一次會

[Word List]

1. auditorium [ˌɔdə`torɪəm] *n.* 禮堂；會堂
2. continental [ˌkɑntə`nɛntl] *adj.* 歐洲大陸式的
3. faculty [`fæklțɪ] *n.* （大學的）全體教職員
4. quad [kwɑd] *n.* 方院

留學　智慧王

Deans 教務長／院長

大家都知道 professor 是什麼意思，但是 dean 又是指誰呢？Dean 是指系所或學院中負責管理行政事務的人。大學中有很多的 dean，每個人各司其職。比如，college dean（院長）會協助你解決學業上的問題。有的 dean 則負責管理學生事務，例如有專門負責校內所有非裔美籍學生事務的 dean。Dean 是很好的資源，他們的主要工作之一就是要幫助學生順利完成大學教育。

Hosts 招待員

有些外籍學生很幸運，因為他們可以分配到招待員。學生招待員由高年級生（upperclassmen）擔任，專門照顧新進的外籍學生，帶他們認識學校，並傾聽他們的問題。社區招待員（community hosts）則由住在學校附近社區的人擔任（但他們可能和學校沒有關係）。他們主要的任務是幫助外籍學生適應美國生活，幫助他們熟悉環境。他們會定期邀請學生到家裡吃午餐或晚餐，看他們是否趕得上學校的進度。如果你有機會分配到招待員，這可是個認識新朋友的好管道，遇到問題時也會有人幫忙。

Jobs 工作

按規定，一般除了在暑假或寒假時到某家公司接受選擇性實習（Optional Practical Training，簡稱 OPT）外，所有的外籍學生都只能在校內工作，但所有的外籍學生在畢業後都可從事為期一年的選擇性實習。研究生可以當教授的助教，職責包括改考卷或報告，或者在討論會中根據某個課程的內容，帶領學生做討論。當助教不限於在自己的系所。許多外籍學生攻讀某個學科，卻當另一系所的助教，例如許多台灣研究生就會當中文助教。你也可以申請圖書館、餐廳或行政辦公室的工作。大學部學生的工作機會可能就侷限於這類工作

了。如果你的經濟狀況穩定，或許就該專心唸書，多參與學校活動，而不是到處打工。

Places on Campus 校內設施 CD 1-08

- graduate research library [ˋgrædʒu͵et ˋrisɝtʃ ͵laɪbrɛrɪ] n. 研究圖書館
- engineering library [͵ɛndʒəˋnɪrɪŋ ͵laɪbrɛrɪ]　　　n. 工程圖書館
- undergraduate library [͵ʌndɚˋgrædʒu͵et ͵laɪbrɛrɪ]　n. 大學部圖書館
- film library [ˋfɪlm ͵laɪbrɛrɪ]　　　　　　　　　n. 電影圖書館
- student union [ˋstjudn̩t ˋjunjən]　　　　　　　n. 學生聯會
- chancellor's complex [ˋtʃænsələz ˋkamplɛks]　　n. 校長辦公大樓
- physical plant [ˋfɪzɪkl̩ ˋplænt]　　　　　　　　n. 設施維護部
- faculty club [ˋfækl̩tɪ ͵klʌb]　　　　　　　　　n. 教職員俱樂部
- natatorium [͵netəˋtorɪəm]　　　　　　　　　　n. 游泳池（尤指室內）
- university art gallery [͵junəˋvɝsətɪ ˋart ͵gælərɪ]　n. 大學附屬美術館
- international center [͵ɪntɚˋnæʃən̩l ˋsɛntɚ]　　　n. 國際中心

People on Campus 校園人物　　　　　　　CD 1-09

- transfer student [ˋtrænsfɚ ͵stjudn̩t]　　　　　n. 轉學生
- re-entry student [riˋɛntrɪ ͵stjudn̩t]　　　　　n. 重入境的留學生
- activist [ˋæktɪvɪst]　　　　　　　　　　　　n. 行動主義者；活躍的人
- performance artist [pɚˋfɔrməns ͵artɪst]　　　n. 表演藝術家
- groundskeeper [ˋgraʊndz͵kipɚ]　　　　　　　n. 校園管理員
- outreach student [ˋaʊtritʃ ͵stjudn̩t]　　　　　n. 校外服務生
- political dissident [pəˋlɪtɪkl̩ ˋdɪsədənt]　　　n. 持不同政治理念的人
- librarian [laɪˋbrɛrɪən]　　　　　　　　　　　n. 圖書館員
- administrator [ədˋmɪnə͵stretɚ]　　　　　　　n. 行政人員
- postdoc [͵postˋdak]　　　　　　　　　　　　n. 博士後研究人員
- homeless person [ˋhomlɪs ˋpɝsn̩]　　　　　　n. 遊民

Chapter 2

Housing 住的問題

Where am I going to live?

Most schools require that first-year students—or freshmen as they're usually called—live in dormitories. This gives freshmen the opportunity to meet people and get settled in very quickly. Dorms in each school are different, but they do tend to follow a basic idea: two people living in one room, sharing a bathroom and other rooms. For graduate students, school apartments are an option, but off-campus housing is usually more popular.

我該住哪裡？

大部分的學校規定一年級生（通常稱為新鮮人）要住宿，如此一來新生就有機會認識朋友，很快地熟悉環境。每所學校的宿舍不同，但都傾向遵循一個基本概念：二人住一寢，共用一間浴室和其他房間。研究生可選擇住學校的公寓，不過他們大多喜歡在校外租房子。

Top 10 必會字彙

 CD **1-10**

★ **balcony**
[`bælkənɪ]

n. 陽台

★ **fireplace**
[`faɪr͵ples]

n. 壁爐

★ **furnished**
[`fɝnɪʃd]

adj. 附家具的

★ **oven**
[`ʌvən]

n. 烤箱

★ **super**
[`supɚ]

n. 管理員
(=superintendent [͵supərɪn`tɛndənt])

★ **washing machine**
[`waʃɪŋ mə͵ʃin]

n. 洗衣機

★ **dryer**
[`draɪɚ]

n. 烘乾機

★ **laundry room**
[`lɔndrɪ ͵rum]

n. 洗衣房

★ **communal bathroom**
[`kamjʊnḷ `bæθ͵rum]

n. 公共浴室

★ **shower caddy**
[`ʃauɚ ͵kædɪ]

n. 盥洗用具籃

CD **1-11**

1 A: Does the apartment have a balcony?

B: Yes it does. And it also has a fireplace. Plus, it's furnished.

A: 這間公寓有陽台嗎？

B: 有的，還有壁爐，而且附家具。

---

2 A: There's something wrong with the oven. I think it's broken.

B: Let's call the super so he can fix it.

A: 烤箱有問題。我想是壞了。

B: 我們打電話給管理員，這樣他就可以來修了。

---

3 A: Where are the washing machine and dryer?

B: In the laundry room down the hall.

A: 洗衣機和烘乾機在哪兒？

B: 在走道後邊的洗衣房裡。

---

4 A: I have to carry so many toiletries each time I go to the communal bathroom.

B: Just buy a shower caddy. You can find them at the student store.

A: 每次去公用浴室，我都得帶一大堆盥洗用具。

B: 買一個盥洗用具籃就好啦。你可以在學生商店買到。

你可以跟我這樣說

CD 1-12

Dialogue A

Annie, a Taiwanese undergrad, is moving into her dorm room at school. Liz, her roommate, has just arrived.

Liz: Hi, you must be my roommate, Annie.

Annie: Hi, and you must be Liz. Nice to finally meet you!

Liz: Nice to meet you, too. After e-mailing all summer, it's great to actually be talking face-to-face!

Annie: I know! I hope you don't mind, but I took the bed on the right.

Liz: Oh, that's fine. My parents should be up in a minute. They're just getting the mini-fridge.

Annie: I've already started putting my clothes in the closet. I thought you could have the right side since it's closer to your bed.

Liz: Great. How about those drawers?

Annie: Well, there are four of them, so you can take the top two, and I'll take the bottom two.

Liz: Do you mind if I take the desk at the foot of my bed?

Annie: Sure, no problem. But all the shelves are above my desk. Feel free to put stuff on them, if you want.

Liz: Thanks! Maybe we can put my stereo up there. You can use it anytime you like.

Annie: Cool. I think our room is going to look great!

安妮，一個來自台灣的大學生，正搬入學校宿舍。她的室友莉姿剛到。

莉姿：嗨，妳一定就是我的室友安妮。

安妮：嗨，那妳一定是莉姿囉。很高興終於見到了妳！

莉姿：我也很高興跟妳見面。通了一整個暑假的電子郵件之後，能真正跟妳面
對面聊幾句真棒！

安妮：可不是！希望妳不會介意，我已經選了右邊的床。

莉姿：哦，不要緊。我爸媽應該馬上就上來了，他們去搬迷你冰箱。

安妮：我已經開始把衣服放進衣櫥裡了。右邊的衣櫥離妳的床比較近，我想就
給妳用。

莉姿：太好了。那些抽屜呢？

安妮：嗯，一共有四個抽屜，妳可以用上面兩個，我用下面兩個好了。

莉姿：妳不介意我選我床尾的那張書桌吧？

安妮：當然，沒問題。不過書架都在我的書桌上方，如果妳要的話，儘管把東
西放在上面。

莉姿：謝了！或許我們可以把我的音響放在上面。妳隨時想用都可以用。

安妮：酷。我們的房間看起來一定會很棒！

[Words & Phrases]

- undergrad [ˋʌndəˏgræd] *n.* 大學生
  （=undergraduate）
- dorm [dɔrm] *n.* 宿舍（=dormitory）
- mini-fridge [ˋmɪnɪ ˏfrɪʤ] *n.* 迷你冰箱
  （又稱 compact refrigerator）
- closet [ˋklɑzɪt] *n.* 衣櫥；櫥櫃
- drawers [drɔəz] *n.* 有抽屜的櫃子（又稱
  chest of drawers）
- foot of the bed　床尾
- stereo [ˋstɛrɪo] *n.* 立體音響

你可以跟我這樣說

CD **1-13**

Dialogue B

Kevin, a graduate student from Taiwan, has come to look at an apartment.

Kevin: Hi, my name is Kevin. I'm here to see the one-bedroom apartment.

Landlord: Hi, Kevin. Nice to meet you. I'm Sally Kestner. The apartment is on the 3rd floor. Let's go take a look!

Kevin: Are most of these apartments occupied by students?

Landlord: Pretty much all of the people here are grad students. It's a great place to live. We're only a ten-minute walk to the main campus. There are also some great restaurants and shops nearby. Here we are! So here's the living room and kitchen. The bedroom is back there, and that's where you'll find the bathroom.

Kevin: Is there air-conditioning?

Landlord: Yes, there's central A/C and heating.

Kevin: Are utilities included in the rent?

Landlord: Yes, they are. That includes water, electricity, and gas.

Kevin: How many phone jacks are there? Is DSL available?

Landlord: There are two phone jacks, one in the living room and one in the bedroom. All apartments are wired for DSL. You just need to call and set up your account.

Kevin: There's a one-year lease, correct? And when is rent due? Is there a security deposit?

Landlord: That's right, you must sign a one-year lease. Rent is due on the 1st of each month. The best thing to do is to mail me a check. And yes, there's a security deposit of two month's rent, which will be returned to you at the end of your lease. Any other questions?

Kevin: Just one. When can I move in?

凱文，一位來自台灣的研究生來看一間公寓。

凱文：嗨，我叫凱文。我是來看有獨立臥房公寓的。

房東：嗨，凱文，很高興認識你。我是莎莉‧凱斯納。那間公寓在三樓，我們
　　　去看看吧！

凱文：這裡的公寓住的大部分都是學生嗎？

房東：這裡的房客幾乎全都是研究生。住這裡很棒，離主校園走路只要十分
　　　鐘，附近也有幾家很不錯的餐廳和商店。到了！客廳和廚房在這裡，臥
　　　室在後面，浴室呢，就在那邊。

凱文：有冷氣嗎？

房東：有，有中央空調的冷暖氣。

凱文：房租有包含水電嗎？

房東：是的，都包含在裡面，包括水費、電費和瓦斯費。

凱文：電話線孔有幾個？有沒有裝 DSL？

房東：有兩個電話線孔，一個在客廳，另一個在臥室。所有的公寓房間都裝了
　　　DSL，只要打電話設定好帳戶就可以用了。

凱文：租約是一年，對嗎？什麼時候要繳房租？需不需要押金？

房東：沒錯，必須簽一年的約。房租每個月的一號要繳，最好是寄支票給我。
　　　還有，沒錯，要兩個月押金，等租約到期後就會還給你。還有其他問題
　　　嗎？

凱文：只有一個。我什麼時候可以搬進來？

[Words & Phrases]

- one-bedroom apartment [ˈwʌn ˈbɛd͵rum əˈpɑrtmənt] *n.* 有獨立一間臥室的公寓
- landlord [ˈlænd͵lɔrd] *n.* 房東；（旅館等）主人；地主
- air-conditioning [ˈɛr kənˈdɪʃənɪŋ] *n.* 空氣調節（= A/C）
- utilities [juˈtɪlətɪz] *n.* （複數）水電等公共設施

- phone jack [ˈfon ͵dʒæk] *n.* 電話線孔
- wired [waɪrd] *adj.* 裝了電線的
- set up 設立
- account [əˈkaʊnt] *n.* 帳戶；戶頭
- lease [lis] *n.* 租賃契約
- due [du] *adj.* 到期的；應給付的
- security deposit [sɪˈkjurətɪ dɪˈpɑzɪt] *n.* 押金

留學 超實用單字

 CD **1-14**

Dorm Life 宿舍生活

★ bathrobe [`bæθ,rob] *n.* 浴袍

You: I'm not used to sharing the bathroom with so many people.
Roommate: Just make sure you wear your bathrobe when you come out of the shower!

你：   我不習慣和一大堆人共用浴室。
室友：   洗完澡之後，只要記得穿好浴袍就行了！

★ Ethernet [`iθɚnɛt] *n.* 乙太網路

Roommate: I love Ethernet! Our Internet connection is so fast.
You: I know! I hear that next year all the dorms are going wireless.[1]

室友：   我愛死乙太網路了！我們的網路速度好快。
你：   可不是！聽說明年所有的宿舍都可無線上網呢。

★ voicemail [`vɔɪs,mel] *n.* 語音信箱

You: Did you check our voicemail?
Roommate: Yup, you got a message from your mom. I saved the message so you can listen to it.

你：   你查過語音信箱了嗎？
室友：   查了，你媽有留言給你。我有保留下來給你聽。

[Word List]

1. wireless [`waɪrlɪs] *adj.* 無線的

★ cable TV [ˋkebḷ ˋtiˋvi] *n.* 有線電視

You: I love watching the TV shows on Comedy Central.
Roommate: Then you'd better sign up for cable TV.

你： 我最喜歡看中央喜劇台的節目。
室友： 那你最好裝有線電視。

★ hot water pot [ˋhat ˋwatɚ ˏpat] *n.* 熱水壺

You: Can I borrow your hot water pot? I want to make some tea.
Roommate: Sure. Could you also boil some extra water for me as well?

你： 你的熱水壺可不可以借我？我想泡茶。
室友： 沒問題。可不可以也順便幫我煮一點熱水？

Apartments and Off-Campus Housing 公寓和校外公寓

★ studio apartment [ˋstjudɪˏo əˏpartmənt] *n.* 單房共用公寓（指共用房間、客廳）

Landlord: Are you looking for a one-bedroom or a studio apartment?
You: My budget[1] is a little tight,[2] so I think a studio will do.

房東： 你要找有獨立臥房的公寓還是單房共用的公寓？
你： 我的預算不多，我想單房共用公寓就好。

[Word List]

1. budget [ˋbʌdʒɪt] *n.* 預算

2. tight [taɪt] *adj.* 緊縮的

CD **1-15**

⭐ long distance / international calls [`lɔŋ `dɪstəns / ˌɪntɚˈnæʃənḷ `kɔlz] *n.* 長途 / 國際電話

You:	I'd like to be able to make long distance and international calls. What would be the best plan for me?
Customer Service:	We have a plan that costs $20 a month. It allows you to make unlimited[1] long distance calls in the United States. For international calls, which country would you be calling?

你：	我想打長途電話跟國際電話，哪種方案最適合我？
客服專員：	我們有個每月 20 美元的方案，您可以打美國國內長途電話，不限次數。至於國際電話，您會打到哪一個國家呢？

⭐ satellite TV [`sætḷˌaɪt `ti `vi] *n.* 衛星電視

Landlord:	Some people here have satellite TV. You can watch every show that's on TV, and all the movie channels.[2]
You:	I think basic cable is all I need.

房東：	這裡有些人有衛星電視，每一個電視節目都收看得到，所有的電影台也都收看得到。
你：	我想我只需要基本的有線電視。

[Word List]

1. unlimited [ʌnˈlɪmɪtɪd] *adj.* 無限制的   2. channel [`tʃænḷ] *n.* 頻道

★ **recyclable** [rɪˋsaɪkləbl̩] *adj.* / *n.* **可回收利用的（東西）**

You:　　　Is there a recycling program in this area?

Landlord: Yes. Separate you recyclables and put them in the marked containers[1] downstairs.

你：　　　這地區有回收計畫嗎？

房東：　　有。分好你可回收的垃圾，把他們放在樓下標示好的箱子裡。

★ **security gate** [sɪˋkjʊrətɪ ˌget] *n.* **安全門**

You:　　　Hi. This is Bernice Chiu. The buzzer[2] on the security gate isn't working.

Landlord: OK. Thanks for calling. I'll send someone out to repair[3] it.

你：　　　喂。我是伯妮絲・邱。安全門上的警報器不會響。

房東：　　好。謝謝妳打電話來。我會派人去修。

★ **hot water heater** [ˋhɑt ˋwɑtɚ ˌhitɚ] *n.* **熱水器**

Landlord: So, you said you were having a problem with the hot water?

You:　　　Yes, I think the hot water heater is broken. Can you send someone to fix it?

房東：　　你說熱水有問題？

你：　　　對，我想熱水器壞了。你可以派人來修嗎？

[Word List]

1. container [kənˋtenɚ] *n.* 容器（如箱、盒、罐等）

2. buzzer [ˋbʌzɚ] *n.* 汽笛；警報器

3. repair [rɪˋpɛr] *v.* 修理；修補

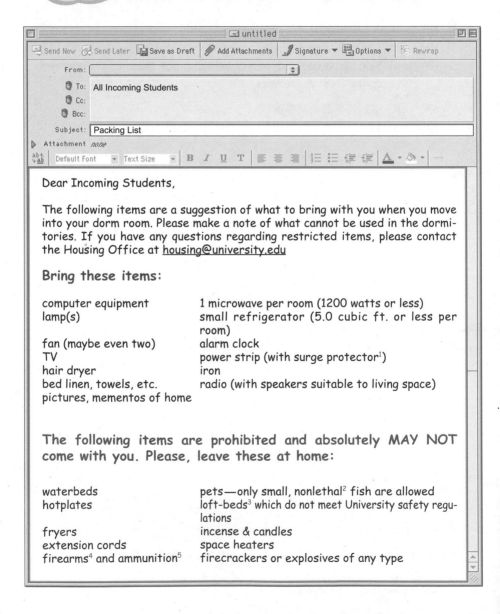

留學 佈告欄

---

untitled

Send Now   Send Later   Save as Draft   Add Attachments   Signature ▼   Options ▼   Rewrap

From:

To: All Incoming Students
Cc:
Bcc:

Subject: Packing List

Attachment *none*

Default Font ▼   Text Size ▼   B *I* U T   ≡ ≡ ≡   ≡ ≡ ≡ ≡   A ▼ ◇ ▼

Dear Incoming Students,

The following items are a suggestion of what to bring with you when you move into your dorm room. Please make a note of what cannot be used in the dormitories. If you have any questions regarding restricted items, please contact the Housing Office at housing@university.edu

Bring these items:

computer equipment	1 microwave per room (1200 watts or less)
lamp(s)	small refrigerator (5.0 cubic ft. or less per room)
fan (maybe even two)	alarm clock
TV	power strip (with surge protector[1])
hair dryer	iron
bed linen, towels, etc.	radio (with speakers suitable to living space)
pictures, mementos of home	

The following items are prohibited and absolutely MAY NOT come with you. Please, leave these at home:

waterbeds	pets—only small, nonlethal[2] fish are allowed
hotplates	loft-beds[3] which do not meet University safety regulations
fryers	incense & candles
extension cords	space heaters
firearms[4] and ammunition[5]	firecrackers or explosives of any type

[翻 譯]

親愛的新生：

以下為遷入宿舍時建議攜帶之物品。請注意，某些物品不可在宿舍內使用，如對禁用物品有任何疑問，請與宿舍辦公室聯絡：housing@university.edu

可攜帶之物品：

電腦設備　　　　　　　　每間房間可使用微波爐乙個（1200 瓦以下）
檯燈（多個可）　　　　　小冰箱（每房間 5.0 立方呎以下）
電扇（二個亦可）　　　　鬧鐘
電視　　　　　　　　　　多孔插座（附穩壓器）
吹風機　　　　　　　　　熨斗
床單、毛巾等　　　　　　收音機（喇叭適合房間大小者）
照片、家庭紀念物品

以下為禁用物品，絕對不可攜帶進入宿舍。請將這些物品留在家裡：

水床　　　　　　　　　　寵物——僅小型無害的魚類可
加熱板　　　　　　　　　不符合學校安全規定之床架
煎鍋　　　　　　　　　　香和蠟燭
延長線　　　　　　　　　暖爐
槍枝和彈藥　　　　　　　炮竹和任何爆裂物品

[Word List]

1. surge protector [ˋsɝdʒ prəˋtɛktɚ] n.
   穩壓器
2. nonlethal [nɑnˋliθəl] adj. 不致命的
3. loft-bed [ˋlɔft ˌbɛd] n. 一種床架（床在
   上面，下面可放桌子等的架子）
4. firearm [ˋfaɪrˌɑrm] n. 火器；槍枝
5. ammunition [ˌæmjəˋnɪʃən] n. 彈藥；
   軍火

留學 智慧王

Dorm Rooms 宿舍房間

每所大學的學生宿舍都不同，不過最常見的兩種是走廊式宿舍（hallway-style dorms）和套房式宿舍（suite-style dorms）。

走廊式宿舍通常是男女同棟（co-ed，意即男女住在同一棟樓中），但分層住。二人住一間，每層樓則共用一間浴室。套房宿舍則是有多個臥房的大房間，大家共用一間客廳、一間浴室。一般而言兩人住一間臥房。

有的宿舍也附有以下設備：
★ 電腦室（computer lab）
★ 讀書室（study room）
★ 洗衣房（laundry room）
★ 共用浴室（communal bathroom）
★ 點心吧（snack bar）
★ 郵件室（mail room）

Roommate Issues 室友問題

很多人從來沒有和室友同住的經驗。有的宿舍提供單人房，但不普遍。有個室友很有趣，但有時也很麻煩，尤其當兩個人的習慣和作息非常不同的時候，更容易產生摩擦。有的學校會請學生填寫表格，列出喜好的室友類型，然後為學生配對，找最適合的室友。以下提供一些小秘訣，讓你和室友相處愉快。

1 如果在開學前就知道室友是誰，可以先寫電子郵件或打電話給對方。在搬進宿舍之前，對未來將共處一室的人有所瞭解，對你百利而無一害！

2　搬進宿舍是一項大工程，搞不好還可能是你這輩子最累的一天。記住，當天大家都很興奮、疲憊和緊張，所以態度要友善，可是不要期待和室友能馬上就一見如故。

3　要互相禮讓！在居住環境狹小，又得和另一個人共用的情況下，應多設身處地為對方著想。注意自己的行為，不要妨礙到對方。舉個例子來說，如果你知道室友習慣早睡，時間到了就不要放音樂，或者講電話。

4　打開天窗說亮話！如果有不滿的情緒，最糟糕的莫過於放在心裡不說出來，這只會讓你越想越氣。應心平氣和地和對方解釋生氣的原因，最好能夠雙方各退讓一步。

5　和同一間套房的人或其他房間的人交朋友。記住，你不需和室友成為知交，也可以住得很開心。

On-Campus/Off-Campus Housing 住校 / 在校外租公寓

　　大部分的學校會提供高年級生（二、三、四年級）和研究生校園公寓。這些公寓一般離校本部很近，房租也比校外的公寓便宜。只可惜有些學校的房間有限，因此研究生大多在校外租房子。有的公寓大樓（apartment complex）或房東僅出租房間給研究生。

Chapter 3

Setting Up House

安頓新家

So I've moved in ... what's next?

If you're living in a dorm or in on-campus housing, moving in is pretty simple. If you're renting your own apartment, however, it's a little more complicated. You'll need to set up your utilities, your phone line, and Internet connection. You may also need to buy furniture (if you're renting an unfurnished place), buy a cell phone, and whatever else you might need to settle in and make your new apartment home.

搬入新家之後，接下來該辦哪些事？

如果你是住學校宿舍或校園公寓，搬家很簡單。但如果是在外自己租公寓，就稍微麻煩一點了。你得自己搞定水電瓦斯、電話線、網路線，也可能得自行購買家具（如果租的公寓沒有附家具）、手機，以及其他任何遷入新居所需的物品，好讓新公寓有家的感覺。

Top 10 必會字彙

 CD 1-16

★ **stove**
[stov]
                        n. 爐子

★ **dishwasher**
[`dɪʃ,waʃɚ]
                        n. 洗碗機

★ **rug**
[rʌg]
                        n. 小地毯

★ **silverware**
[`sɪlvɚ,wɛr]
                        n. 銀製食具；餐具

★ **toaster**
[`tostɚ]
                        n. 烤麵包機

★ **carpet**
[`kɑrpɪt]
                        n. 地毯

★ **DustBuster**
[`dʌst,bʌstɚ]
                        n. 手提式吸塵器

★ **slob**
[slɑb]
                        n. 邋遢鬼

★ **common room**
[`kɑmən ,rum]
                        n. 公用休息室；交誼廳

★ **inconsiderate**
[,ɪnkən`sɪdərɪt]
                        adj. 不懂為他人著想的

CD **1-17**

1 A: The kitchen has a refrigerator, stove, and a dishwasher.

B: Great. I'll buy a little rug to put on the floor by the sink.

A: 廚房有冰箱、爐子和洗碗機。

B: 太好了。我會買一個小地毯，鋪在靠洗碗槽的地板上。

---

2 A: I bought some silverware. Now all we need is a toaster.

B: Should we get a regular toaster, or a toaster oven?

A: 我買了一些銀製餐具，現在只需再買個烤麵包機就行了。

B: 我們要買普通的烤麵包機，還是小型烤箱？

---

3 A: Oh no! I spilled my bag of chips on the carpet.

B: Don't worry. I'll go get the DustBuster to clean it up.

A: 糟了，我把一包洋芋片都灑在地毯上了。

B: 別擔心，我去拿手提式吸塵器來清乾淨。

---

4 A: My roommate is a total slob. She leaves empty food containers everywhere.

B: Leaving messes in the common room is so inconsiderate.

A: 我的室友是個十足的邋遢鬼，她吃完的食物盒到處放。

B: 把交誼廳搞得亂七八糟是非常不為他人著想的行為。

你可以跟我這樣說

 CD 1-18

Dialogue A

Kevin calls his landlord to confirm his move-in date.

Kevin: Hi, Sally. This is Kevin Chen. I'm just calling to confirm that I can move in this Monday, the 18th of August.

Landlord: Hi, Kevin. Thanks for double-checking. That's right, you're moving in on Monday. Do you know what time you'll get here?

Kevin: Probably around 10 a.m. I'd like to get an early start since I have quite a bit to do, and my bed is going to be delivered around that time.

Landlord: No problem. I'll meet you in the parking lot so I can give you your key. Please don't forget your security deposit.

Kevin: I won't. I already had a cashier's check made out. And what about the lease? I haven't signed it yet.

Landlord: Of course! Thanks for reminding me. I'll bring two copies for both of us to sign, and then we'll both have one. Am I forgetting anything else?

Kevin: How about the utilities? Will they be turned on by Monday?

Landlord: Oh, yes. The gas, water, and power will all be ready before you move in. They're all still in my name, so there shouldn't be any problems. By the way, did you take care of the phone?

Kevin: Yes, I did. It's in my name now. The phone company said they'll be by on Wednesday to hook up the DSL.

Landlord: Great! Then I'll see you on Monday.

Kevin: Monday it is. Bye.

凱文打電話給房東，確認遷入日期。

凱文：嗨，莎莉。我是凱文・陳，打電話來跟妳確認這個星期一 8 月 18 號可以搬進來。

房東：嗨，凱文，謝謝你跟我再次確認遷入日期。沒錯，你是要在星期一搬進來。那你幾點會到呢？

凱文：大概早上 10 點左右。我想早一點搬，因為有很多事要做，我的床大概也會在那時候送來。

房東：沒問題。我跟你約在停車場見，以便把鑰匙交給你。請不要忘了帶押金。

凱文：我不會忘記的，銀行本票我都已經開好了。那租約的事情呢？我還沒有簽名。

房東：當然，當然！謝謝你提醒我。我會帶兩份合約給雙方簽名，然後各執一份。我還有沒有什麼漏掉的？

凱文：那水電瓦斯呢？禮拜一就都可以用了嗎？

房東：喔，對。水電瓦斯在你搬進來之前就都會搞定，它們都還登記在我名下，所以不會有問題的。對了，你電話申請了嗎？

凱文：申請了，是用我的名字。電信公司說他們禮拜三會過來裝 DSL。

房東：太好了！那禮拜一見囉。

凱文：就禮拜一了。掰。

[Words & Phrases]

- confirm [kən`fɝm] *v.* 確認
- double-check [`dʌbḷ `tʃɛk] *v.* 仔細複核；再次檢查
- parking lot [`pɑrkɪŋ ˌlɑt] *n.* 停車場
- cashier's check [kæ`ʃɪrz ˌtʃɛk] *n.* 銀行本票
- hook up 接線

你可以跟我這樣說

 CD **1-19**

Dialogue B

Annie is adjusting to life with a roommate.

Annie: Hey Liz, I'm really sorry, but I can't concentrate on my reading with the music so loud.

Liz: Oh, sorry. I'll turn off the stereo.

Annie: No, you can still listen to music. But it would be great if you could just turn it down.

Liz: No problem. *(Liz goes to the refrigerator to get some water.)* Hey, Annie, could you please fill up the water filter when you finish the water? It's kind of a pain to find it empty all the time.

Annie: Of course. I'm sorry about that. Um ... do you know what happened to the leftover takeout in the fridge?

Liz: Oh, I ate it. Sorry, I thought you said to help myself. I'll make sure next time.

Annie: No worries. I guess I forgot.

Liz: Are you sure it's okay? I'm getting the feeling that you're annoyed with me.

Annie: No, I'm not. I guess I'm just not used to having a room-mate. I'm sorry if I sounded upset.

Liz: It's okay. It's a bit hard for me, too. Why don't we go to the snack bar and talk about what we can do to make our living situation easier?

Annie: Sure, great idea.

安妮正在適應有室友的生活。

安妮：嘿，莉姿，真不好意思，但是妳音樂開得那麼大聲，我沒辦法專心看書。

莉姿：哦，對不起，我這就把音響關掉。

安妮：不，妳還是可以聽音樂，只要關小聲一點就好了。

莉姿：沒問題。（*莉姿到冰箱拿水喝。*）嘿，安妮，過濾瓶的水要是喝完了，能不能把水重新裝滿？每次要喝水的時候都沒水，有一點討厭。

安妮：當然可以。對不起。呃……妳知不知道冰箱裡剩下的外帶食物到哪裡去了？

莉姿：哦，我吃掉了。抱歉，我以為妳說我可以吃。下次我會注意。

安妮：沒關係。我想是我忘了。

莉姿：妳確定沒關係嗎？我覺得妳好像對我有一點不爽快。

安妮：沒有，我沒有不爽。我想我只是還不習慣和室友住吧。如果我口氣不好，對不起。

莉姿：沒關係，我也覺得和室友住不容易。我們何不到點心吧去談一談該怎麼做才能讓住一起的生活好過一點？

安妮：好啊，好主意。

[Words & Phrases]

- turn down 調低（音量、冷氣等）
- water filter [ˋwɑtɚ͵fɪltɚ] *n.* 濾水器
- pain [pen] *n.* 苦惱
- leftover [ˋlɛft͵ovɚ] *adj.* 剩下的；未用完的
- takeout [ˋtek͵aut] *n.* 外帶的食物
- annoyed [əˋnɔɪd] *adj.* 感到困擾的；感到討厭的
- living situation [ˋlɪvɪŋ͵sɪtʃuˋeʃən] *n.* 生活狀態

留學 超實用單字

CD 1-20

Settling Into Your Apartment 安頓新家

★ lamp [læmp] *n.* 檯燈

Landlord: The bedroom doesn't have a lot of natural lighting.[1]
You: That's okay. I'll just buy a few lamps.

房東： 這間臥房自然採光不多。
你：   沒關係。我買幾盞檯燈就好了。

② bathtub [`bæθ,tʌb] *n.* 浴缸

You: The best thing about my apartment is my bathtub. I love taking long baths.
Friend: You're lucky. I only have a shower[2] in my apartment.

你：   我的公寓中最棒的就是浴缸。我最喜歡泡久久的澡 。
朋友： 你真幸運。我的公寓只有淋浴設備。

③ courtyard [`kort,jard] *n.* 庭院

Landlord: When the weather is nice, the people in this apartment complex[3] get together and have a barbecue in the courtyard.
You: With so many people in this complex, does it ever get too noisy?

房東： 天氣好的時候，這棟公寓大樓的房客會聚在一起，在院子裡烤肉。
你：   這棟大樓的房客那麼多，會不會變得太吵？

[Word List]

1. natural lighting [`nætʃərəl ,laɪtɪŋ] *n.*
   自然採光

2. shower [`ʃauɚ] *n.* 淋浴設備；淋浴室

3. apartment complex [ə`partmənt kəm`plɛks] *n.* 公寓大樓

★ vacuum cleaner [`vækjʊəm ˌklinɚ] *n.* 吸塵器

You:　　　　Do you know where I can buy a vacuum cleaner?
Landlord:　Just go to Wal-Mart. They have everything there.

你　：　　請問哪裡買得到吸塵器？
房東：　　去 Wal-Mart 就行了，那裡要什麼有什麼。

★ mop [map] *n.* 拖把

You:　　　　The kitchen floor gets really dirty. I need to buy a mop.
Friend:　　You should get that new mop that uses disposable[1] wet
　　　　　　wipes.[2]

你　：　　廚房地板真是髒得可以了。我得買一支拖把。
朋友：　　你應該買那種使用拋棄式溼巾的新式拖把。

Roommates and Dorm Issues 室友和宿舍問題

★ R.A. (= resident advisor [`rɛzədənt ədˌvaɪzɚ]) *n.* 舍監

You:　　　　If we can't solve this problem on our own, we'll have to
　　　　　　talk to our R.A.
Roommate: You're right. We need an unbiased[3] person to help us
　　　　　　decide whose fault it is!

你　：　　我們要是無法自行解決這個問題，就得找舍監談了。
室友：　　說得沒錯。我們需要一個公正的人來定奪，看這是誰的錯！

[**Word List**]

1. disposable [dɪ`spozəbl̩] *adj.* 拋棄式的
2. wet wipe [`wet ˌwaɪp] *n.* 溼巾
3. unbiased [ʌn`baɪəst] *adj.* 公正客觀的

CD 1-21

★ borrow [`baro] *v.* 借

Roommate: Look, I don't mind it if you borrow my stuff. But please ask first!

You: I did! Sorry, I guess you didn't hear me because you were on the phone.

室友： 喂，你要借用我的東西沒關係，但請先問一聲！

你： 我問啦！對不起，我想你大概沒聽到，因為當時你在講電話。

★ compromise [`kamprə,maɪz] *v.* 妥協

You: I really can't get along with[1] my roommate.

R.A.: I know it's hard, but you have to compromise. Why don't you work out[2] an agreement where you don't wake her up too early in the morning, and she doesn't talk on the phone too late at night?

妳： 我和我室友真的處不來。

舍監： 我知道和她相處不容易，不過妳們得各退一步。妳們何不協議一下——妳不要一大早吵醒她，她也不要深更半夜還講電話？

★ vending machine [`vɛndɪŋ ,mə`ʃin] *n.* 自動販賣機

Roommate: I'm going to get a candy bar. Do you want anything from the vending machine?

You: Could you get me a bag of chips?

室友： 我要去買糖果條。要不要我幫你從販賣機買什麼回來？

你： 可不可以幫我買一包洋芋片？

[Word List]

1. get along with sb. 與某人和睦相處　　　2. work out 努力獲致；解決（問題）

★⁵ cleaning staff [`klɪnɪŋ ˌstæf] *n.* 清潔人員

You: The lady who comes to clean our dorm is so nice.

Roommate: The cleaning staff here is great. They're so friendly and they do such a good job of cleaning.

你: 幫我們打掃宿舍的太太人真好。

室友: 這裡的清潔人員很棒。他們人都很友善,而且打掃得很乾淨。

★⁶ padlock [`pædˌlɑk] *n.* 掛鎖（通常為U型）

You: Where should I keep things like valuable[1] documents and my passport?

R.A.: You can get a padlock for your desk and keep them in there.

你: 我要把貴重文件和護照之類的東西放哪兒?

舍監: 你可以找個桌用掛鎖,把東西放那兒。

[Word List]

1. valuable [`væljuəbl] *adj.* 值錢的;貴重的

留學 佈告欄

Things to Do

1) Reconfirm move-in date with landlord
2) Buy a bed and have it delivered to the apartment
3) Set up phone line and DSL
4) Buy bed sheets[1] and towels
5) Buy a cell phone

Things to Do After Moving In

1) Buy kitchenware[2]
2) Buy textbooks
3) Figure out what other furniture I might need

[翻　譯]

待辦事項

1）和房東再次確認遷入日期
2）購買床鋪，請店家送貨
3）加裝電話線和 DSL
4）購買床單和毛巾
5）購買手機

遷入後待辦事項

1）購買廚房用具
2）買上課用書
3）想想看，還需添購哪些家具

[Word List]

1. sheet [ʃit] *n.* 床單

2. kitchenware [ˋkɪtʃɪnˏwɛr] *n.*（總稱）廚房用具

留學　智慧王

Apartment Listings 公寓出租廣告

在你到學校之前，就應該先上網看一看公寓出租的廣告。就算到校之前還沒找到地方住，看一看網路上的廣告，也可以大概了解自己理想中的公寓該是什麼樣子、房租會是多少，以及房子容不容易找。

大學裡面都有佈告欄，上面會張貼公寓或房子的出租廣告。當地報紙或校刊上的分類廣告也是很理想的資訊來源。不要忘了，很多地方在暑假開始之前就會被租走了。盡量提早到學校，這樣你才有充裕的時間找地方住、安頓下來並準備開學。你也可以和其他的台灣學生聊一聊，請教相關事宜。

Furniture 家具

購買家具時，沒有必要全都買新的。如果你租的公寓有附家具，只要購買幾樣，如書桌即可。當地也一定有販賣二手家具的地方。若有意購買此類家具，可以看一下學校報紙，或者留意拍賣二手家具的傳單和告示牌。

Computers 電腦

大部分的留學生喜歡使用手提電腦（laptops），以便隨身攜帶到處跑。大學生在課堂上通常用不到手提電腦，多數人仍然喜歡動手做筆記，不過桌上型電腦（tablet PCs）越來越受理工科學生的歡迎。研究生則經常使用手提電腦，甚至會在上課時使用。

所有的圖書館都會附設電腦區（computer areas），校園各個地方一般也會設有電腦室（computer labs），有的甚至一天二十四小時開放使用。如果你比較喜歡使用自己的手提電腦，大多數的大學如今也都設有無線網路（Wi-

Fi）。一般而言，無線網路通常設在圖書館和教室大樓中，不過有的學校會在戶外設置無線網路，讓學生享受戶外無線上網的樂趣。

Bed Linens and Others Things 床單和其他相關物品

無論你是大學部還是碩、博士班學生，到國外留學都可能令人感到害怕，尤其如果是自己一個人出國，還只能帶兩件行李上飛機，更是叫人膽怯！床單和其他房間或公寓所需的物品，可以等到了目的地之後再行購買。床單、毛巾和盥洗用品等在大型賣場如 Target、Kmart、Wal-Mart，或者像 Bed, Bath and Beyond 等商店都買得到。在搬家之前就盡量把這些東西買齊全，這樣一來，搬入新家的第一晚你就可以安安穩穩地入睡了。

Dealing with an Impossible Roommate 和難纏室友的相處之道

幾乎所有的大學都規定一年級生要住校，因此會在每一棟宿舍大樓中安排一位舍監（R.A.）。舍監多為高年級生，專門為一年級的新生解決各種疑難雜症，並幫忙解決室友間的問題。

大部分的人不習慣和別人一起生活，對某些人而言，甚至會很痛苦。若你的生活狀況變得難以忍受，最好馬上找舍監談談。如果情況仍然不見改善，大部分學校會接受更換房間的申請。不過何時才能換房間，得視你何時提出申請而定；一般可能需要一段時間才能如願，如果太晚申請，甚至可能沒辦法換。

如果不幸得和全世界最糟糕的室友住在同一房間，該怎麼辦？你可以先和對方談一談，看看是否可以各自退讓一步。要是問題還是不能解決，再找舍監幫忙協調。真到非不得已的時候，再申請換房間。很多人和室友相處並不融洽，但是大學生活仍過得多采多姿。千萬不要因為一個差勁的室友而破壞了你美好的留學經驗。

CD 1-22

Cleaning/Repairing/Maintaining Your Place 打掃／修理／維持自己的窩

- steam clean the carpet　　　　　　　　用蒸汽清理地毯
- touch up the walls　　　　　　　　　　修補牆壁
- spackle [`spɑkḷ]　　　　　　　　　　　（建）填泥料
- repaint [ri`pent]　　　　　　　　　　　重新油漆、粉刷
- re-key the locks　　　　　　　　　　　更換鎖
- replace a light bulb [`laɪt ˌbʌlb]　　　更換燈泡
- fix a water leak [lik]　　　　　　　　　修理漏水
- clean the sink trap [`sɪŋk ˌtræp]　　　清理洗滌槽濾網
- mow [mo] the lawn　　　　　　　　　除草
- spray for fleas [fliz]　　　　　　　　　噴灑跳蚤藥

Chapter 4

Social Security Number, Banking, and Money

社會安全號碼、與銀行往來及金錢

How do I pay for everything?

One of the first things you need to do is open a bank account. Choose a bank with many branches to make it easier for you to find an ATM. Some banks will require that you have a Social Security Number before you can open a bank account; however, major banks, such as Bank of America, only require foreign nationals to provide their passport. Most international students will first bring a small amount of cash and traveler's checks to get settled in, and then have money wired to their bank account.

我該怎麼付錢？

出國後馬上要辦的一件事就是開立銀行帳戶。最好選一家分行多的銀行，這樣找提款機時會比較方便。開戶時，有的銀行會要求你提供社會安全號碼，不過規模較大的銀行，如美國銀行，只要求外籍人士提供護照就可以開戶。大部分的外籍學生會先攜帶一點現金和旅行支票開戶，之後再把錢匯進帳戶裡。

Top 10 必會字彙

 CD **1-23**

★ **withdrawal**   *n.* 提款
[wɪðˋdrɔəl]

★ **fee**   *n.* 費用；手續費
[fi]

★ **personal identification number (PIN)**   *n.* 密碼
[ˋpɝsn̩l aɪˌdɛntəfəˋkeʃən ˌnʌmbɚ]

★ **checkbook**   *n.* 支票簿
[ˋtʃɛkˌbʊk]

★ **reorder**   *v.* 再訂貨
[riˋɔrdɚ]

★ **bounce**   *v.* 跳票
[baʊns]

★ **deposit slip**   *n.* 存款單
[dɪˋpazɪt ˌslɪp]

★ **part-time**   *adj.* 兼職的
[ˋpɑrt ˌtaɪm]

★ **visa status**   *n.* 簽證資格
[ˋvizə ˋstetəs]

★ **eligible**   *adj.* 符合資格的
[ˋɛlɪdʒəbl̩]

CD 1-24

1 A: I'm out of money. I need to go to the bank and make a withdrawal.

B: Why don't you just go to an ATM?

A: Because I don't want to pay the ATM fee. Plus, I forgot my PIN!

A: 我沒錢了，得到銀行提款。

B: 為什麼不用提款機就得了？

A: 因為我不想付提款機使用費，況且我也忘了密碼！

---

2 A: Hand me my checkbook. I have to pay the rent. Oh no, I'm out of checks!

B: Looks like it's time to reorder some.

A: 把支票簿拿給我，我必須付房租。糟糕，我的支票用完了！

B: 看來得再訂一些了。

---

3 A: Oh no! My rent check bounced!

B: Get some money and a deposit slip, and put money in your account right away.

A: 糟糕！我開的房租支票跳票了！

B: 拿一些錢和一張存款單，馬上把錢存進銀行帳戶。

---

4 A: I'm interested in some part-time work.

B: OK. We'll have to check your visa status to see if you're eligible.

A: 我想找兼職的工作。

B: 好的。我們得看一看你的簽證，看你是不是符合資格。

你可以跟我這樣說

CD 1-25

Dialogue A

Kevin goes to the Social Security Administration to apply for his SSN.

Kevin: Hello. I'm here to apply for a Social Security Number.

Clerk: Please fill out this form. Have you been in the U.S. for at least ten days?

Kevin: Yes, I got here three weeks ago.

Clerk: I'll need to see your passport, I-94, I-20, and a letter of employment.

Kevin: Here you go. *(Kevin hands all documents to the clerk.)*

Clerk: What employment are you being offered?

Kevin: I'll be working as a teaching assistant for Professor Bloomfield in the engineering department.

Clerk: You also need a letter from your school verifying your legal status.

Kevin: Oops, sorry. Almost forgot about that. Here you go. *(Kevin hands the letter to the clerk.)*

Clerk: I also need to see another form of identification.

Kevin: Another form of I.D.? I don't know if I have one on me.

Clerk: A driver's license, insurance card, or a school I.D. will do.

Kevin: Oh, I have my student I.D. with me.

Clerk: OK, you should get your Social Security card in the mail in about two weeks if the Department of Homeland Security verifies your documents right away.

Kevin: Thanks.

凱文到社會安全福利局申請社會安全號碼。

凱文： 你好，我想申請社會安全號碼。

辦事員：請填寫這張申請表。你已經在美國住十天以上了嗎？

凱文： 是的，我三個星期前來的。

辦事員：我需要看你的護照、I-94、I-20 跟工作證明函。

凱文： 在這裡。（*凱文把所有文件拿給辦事員。*）

辦事員：你將從事什麼樣的工作？

凱文： 我會在工程系擔任布倫菲德教授的助教。

辦事員：我們還需要看你的學校證明，確定你具有合法身份。

凱文： 哎呀，對不起，差一點忘了。在這裡。（*凱文把證明拿給辦事員。*）

辦事員：我還需要看另一種身分證件。

凱文： 另一種身分證件？我不知道我有沒有帶別的證件。

辦事員：駕照、保險卡、或學校證件等都可以。

凱文： 哦，我帶了學生證。

辦事員：好，要是國土安全部能立刻確認你的資料，兩個禮拜之內你就應該會
收到我們寄發的社會安全卡了。

凱文： 謝謝。

[Words & Phrases]

- administration [ədˌmɪnəˋstreʃən] *n.* 行政機構；管理部門
- apply for 申請
- fill out 填寫（表格、文件等）
- I-94 入境／出境記錄表格
- employment [ɪmˋplɔɪmənt] *n.* 職業；工作
- teaching assistant [ˋtitʃɪŋ əˌsɪstənt] *n.* 助教
- verify [ˋvɛrəˌfaɪ] *v.* 證實
- form [fɔrm] *n.* 種類；形式
- identification [aɪˌdɛntəfəˋkeʃən] *n.* 證明

你可以跟我這樣說

 CD **1-26**

Dialogue B

Annie asks how money can be wired into her account.

Clerk: You'll get your checks in the mail in about a week, and your check card should arrive by the end of this month. If you don't receive them, just give us a call. In the meantime, you can use these starter checks. They don't have your name or your address, so you'll have to write your information at the top left-hand corner if you use them.

Annie: I was wondering how money can be wired into my account.

Clerk: Where will it be wired from?

Annie: Taiwan. My parents don't have a bank account in the U.S., so they'll wire me money.

Clerk: You need to give them the routing numbers of our bank. The number under our logo on your checks is our ACH Routing Number. The numbers at the bottom are the ABA Check Routing Number, your account number, and your check number. There's a $20 fee when an international wire is made into your account.

Annie: Will a bank statement be mailed to me every month?

Clerk: Yes, but you can also choose to have it e-mailed to you. Would you prefer that?

Annie: Sure. Thanks for your help!

Clerk: My pleasure. And you'll also be able to access your account online using our website.

Annie: Thank you. Have a great day.

Clerk: You too.

安妮問辦事員如何將錢匯入帳戶。

辦事員：您大約一個禮拜內就會收到支票，支票卡則應該在月底前會收到。如果沒有收到，打給電話給我們即可。在這段期間內您可以先用這些臨時支票。支票上面沒有您的姓名和住址，所以使用時您必須在左上角寫上您的資料。

安妮：　我想知道錢要如何匯進我的帳戶裡？

辦事員：錢會從哪裡匯來？

安妮：　台灣。我父母在美國沒有銀行帳戶，所以他們會把錢匯給我。

辦事員：您得把我們的國際銀行代碼給他們。您的支票上面有我們銀行的商標，下面就是我們的銀行票據交換代碼。支票下方是我們的美國銀行協會轉帳代碼、您的帳號以及支票號碼。由國外匯款進入您的帳戶時，我們會收取 20 美元的費用。

安妮：　銀行明細表會不會每個月寄給我？

辦事員：會，不過您也可以選擇用電子郵件的方式寄給您。您比較喜歡這個方式嗎？

安妮：　好啊。謝謝你的幫忙！

辦事員：這是我的榮幸。您也可以透過我們的網站查閱您的帳戶。

安妮：　謝謝你。祝你有愉快的一天。

辦事員：您也一樣。

[Words & Phrases]

- wire [waɪr] *v.* 電匯
- starter check [`stɑrtɚ ˌtʃɛk] *n.* 臨時支票
- routing number [`rautɪŋ ˌnʌmbɚ] *n.* 國際代碼
- logo [`logo] *n.* 標誌
- ACH (=Automated Clearing House) *n.* 自動票據交換所
- ABA (=American Bankers Association) *n.* 美國銀行協會
- bank statement [`bæŋk ˌstetmənt] *n.* 銀行明細表
- access [`æksɛs] *v.* 取得（資料等）

留學　超實用單字

CD **1-27**

At the Social Security Office 在社會安全福利局

⭐ **terms of employment** [ˋtɝms əv ɪmˋplɔɪmənt] *n.* **雇用條件**

> You: When I apply for a SSN, what does the employment letter need to say?
>
> Clerk: The letter needs to outline the offer and terms of your employment.
>
> 你： 申請社會安全號碼的時候，工作證明函中應該提到些什麼？
>
> 辦事員：函中應該概述工作內容和僱用條件。

⭐ **Employment Authorization Document (EAD)** [ɪmˋplɔɪmənt ͵ɔθərəˋzeʃən ˋdakjəmənt] *n.* **工作許可證**

> You: I'm going to work over the summer. What documents do I need if I'm applying for Optional[1] Practical Training—OPT?
>
> Clerk: You can submit an Employment Authorization Document instead of a letter of employment.
>
> 你： 暑假時我打算工作。如果我要申請選擇性實習，需要準備哪些文件？
>
> 辦事員：您不需繳工作證明信函，只要有工作許可證就可以了。

Banking 與銀行往來

⭐ **checking account** [ˋtʃɛkɪŋ əˋkaʊnt] *n.* **支票帳戶**

> You: Hi. I'd like to open a checking account.
>
> Clerk: Here's a brochure[2] that outlines the different kinds of checking accounts we have.
>
> 你： 嗨。我想開一個支票帳戶。
>
> 辦事員：這本小冊子上有我們各種不同支票帳戶的介紹。

[Word List]

1. optional [ˋɑpʃən!] *adj.* 可選擇的

2. brochure [broˋʃʊr] *n.* 小冊子

☆ monthly fee [`mʌnθlɪ `fi] n. 月費

You: Which kind of checking account do you recommend?[1]

Clerk: Our Student Checking Account is a good match for you. There isn't a monthly fee for the first six months.

你: 你會推薦哪種支票帳戶呢？

辦事員：我們的學生支票帳戶很符合您的需求。開戶後的前六個月內不必繳月費。

★ teller visit [`tɛlɚ ˌvɪzɪt] n. 銀行櫃員服務

You: How many teller visits am I allowed each month?

Clerk: You have two teller visits each month. If you go over, each extra visit is $2.

你: 我每個月可以使用幾次櫃員服務？

辦事員：您每個月可以使用兩次。如果超過兩次，每次必須交 2 美元的費用。

★ CD (= Certificate of Deposit [sɚ`tɪfəkɪt əv dɪ`pazɪt]) n. 定存單

You: Do you have any savings accounts with a higher interest rate?

Clerk: You may want to consider opening a CD. The interest is higher, and you can choose terms from one month to ten years.

你: 你們有沒有利息較高的存款帳戶？

辦事員：您可以考慮開個定存帳戶。這種帳戶利息較高，您可以簽一個月到十年的合約。

[Word List]

1. recommend [ˌrɛkə`mɛnd] v. 推薦

CD 1-28

★ account number [əˈkaʊnt ˌnʌmbɚ] *n.* 帳號

Clerk: I'm sorry. I can't tell if this is a one or a seven in your account number.

You: Sorry. I didn't write it clearly. That's a seven.

辦事員：不好意思，我分不太清楚您帳號中的這個是一還是七。

你： 抱歉。我沒有寫清楚，是七。

★ bank branch [ˈbæŋk ˌbræntʃ] *n.* 銀行分行

You: Hello. I'd like to exchange[1] some money.

Clerk: I'm sorry. You'll have to go to our main bank branch for that.

你： 你好。我想要換一些外幣。

辦事員：抱歉。您必須到我們本行去才有那項服務。

★ safety deposit box [ˈseftɪ dɪˈpazɪt ˌbaks] *n.* 保險箱

You: Hello. I'd like to access my safety deposit box. Here's my key.

Clerk: OK. Please sign your name here and I will compare it to the signature[2] on file.

你： 你好。我想要查看我的保險箱，這是我的鑰匙。

辦事員：好。請在這兒簽名，我要拿它跟檔案上的簽名比對一下。

[**Word List**]

1. exchange [ɪksˈtʃendʒ] *v.* 兌換；交換   2. signature [ˈsɪgnətʃɚ] *n.* 簽名

⭐ cashier's check [kæ`ʃɪrz ˌtʃɛk] *n.* 銀行本票

You: Hello. I need to get a cashier's check.

Clerk: OK. For what amount? And who do you want it made payable[1] to?

你： 你好。我想開張銀行本票。

辦事員：好。金額是多少？抬頭人是要寫誰呢？

⭐ check card [`tʃɛk ˌkard] *n.* 支票卡（銀行所發行的一種卡，可於消費時使用，金額會直接從帳戶中扣除）

Clerk: Would you like your photo to be on your check card? It's great for I.D. purposes.

You: Sure. Can you take the photo here, or do I need to supply one?

辦事員：您要不要在支票卡上面放照片？當證件很好用。

你： 好啊。你要當場拍照，還是要我拿張照片來？

[Word List]

1. payable [`peəbḷ] *adj.* 應付的

留學 佈告欄

SOCIAL SECURITY

XXX–XX–XXXX

THIS NUMBER HAS BEEN ESTABLISHED[1] FOR

JONATHAN C SHAW

_____
SIGNATURE

[翻 譯]

社會安全卡

XXX-XX-XXXX
此號碼已建檔給
強納森・查爾斯・蕭

_____
簽名

[Word List]

1. establish [ə`stæblɪʃ] v. 建立

留學 智慧王

Social Security Number (SSN) 社會安全號碼

社會安全福利是美國的社會保險制度，不是一種身分證明的系統。不過美國人在報稅、申請駕照等時候，都會用到社會安全卡。除非你打算在美國工作（多數外籍學生只能在大學內工作，而不能在校外工作），否則不需要申請社會安全號碼。

持有社會安全號碼在生活上會比較方便，但這並不足以構成申請的理由。申請時，社會安全福利局會要求你提供以下證明：
★ 護照和 I-94
★ I-20
★ 美國雇主開立的工作證明函（內容應提到雇用細節）
★ 學校信函，證明你具有合法簽證資格。

Checking Account? Savings Account? 支票帳戶還是存款帳戶好呢？

大部分的學生會開兩種帳戶：支票帳戶（checking account）和存款帳戶（savings account）。有了支票帳戶，便可以開支票，因為大部分的帳單都得用支票付款；有了存款帳戶，則可以賺取存款利息。有的外籍學生只開支票帳戶，然後把每年或每學期會用到的錢匯到戶頭中。

支票帳戶和存款帳戶有很多種類可供選擇。每家銀行的帳戶特色和服務各異；有的會要求最低存款額，若不足額就會按月向你收取管理費用，有的則僅允許有限的櫃員服務，也就是實際到櫃台使用銀行的服務次數。

Checks 支票

支票通常被用來支付房租、水電瓦斯費和信用卡帳單，不過學生之間也會

使用支票。建議你經常注意帳目的平衡（隨時更新存款、開過的支票和提款的紀錄）。大部分的商店只收上面印有姓名、地址和電話的支票。

Check Cards 支票卡

支票卡就跟金融卡一樣，可以用它從提款機提領支票帳戶中的錢。支票卡還有簽帳功能，非常好用。它還與常見的信用卡，例如 Visa 卡結合，買東西時如果該商店接受 Visa 卡，便可使用。如果用支票卡購物，只要在商店鍵入密碼，金額即立刻會從帳戶中扣除。

ATM Banking 提款機服務

如果你使用的是自己銀行的提款機，美國大部分的銀行都不收取服務費；但若是使用其他銀行的提款機，你的銀行和對方銀行都會向你收取服務費。許多美國人喜歡利用提款機處理與銀行往來的事務，不過美國的提款機並不具轉帳功能。由於不能使用提款機繳交各種費用，所以大家都使用支票。

Credit Cards 信用卡

大部分剛到美國的外籍學生都不能申請信用卡，因為他們在美國沒有信用紀錄。有的銀行會提供額度較低的學生信用卡。一旦開始累積良好的信用記錄，便會有比較多的機會申請信用卡。剛出國時，最好帶一張國內的信用卡去，以便緊急時使用。

Paying Your Bills Online 網路繳費

由於美國人不能用提款機繳費，因此網路付款便變得越來越受歡迎。大部

分的人會用網路查閱自己的銀行明細、付卡費和手機費。美國人認為網路銀行夠安全，也使繳費變得更方便。

CD **1-29**

- **Aldine Teachers Credit Union** [ˋɔldin ˋtitʃɚz ˋkrɛdɪt ˏjunjən] 埃爾丁教師信用社
- **Bank of America** [ˋbæŋk əv əˋmɛrɪkə] 美國銀行
- **Bank One** [ˋbæŋk ˋwʌn] 美一銀行
- **JP Morgan Chase Bank** [ˋʤeiˋpi ˋmɔrgən ˋtʃes ˏbæŋk] 摩根大通銀行
- **Citibank** [ˋsɪtɪˏbæŋk] 花旗銀行
- **Downey Federal Credit Union** [ˋdaʊnɪ ˋfɛdərəl ˋkrɜdɪt ˏjunjən] 道尼聯邦信用社
- **First Union Bank** [ˋfɚst ˋjunjən ˏbæŋk] 美聯銀行
- **Skidmore Students Federal Credit Union** [ˋskɪdmor ˏstjudn̩ts ˋfɛdərəl ˋkrɛdɪt ˏjunjən] 斯德摩爾學生聯邦信用社
- **Union Bank** [ˋjunjən ˏbæŋk] 美商聯合銀行
- **Washington Mutual Bank** [ˋwaʃɪŋtən ˋmjutʃʊəl ˏbæŋk] 華盛頓互惠銀行
- **Wells Fargo Bank** [ˋwɛlz ˋfargo ˏbæŋk] 美商富國銀行

Chapter 5

Food and Eating Out

食物和外食

What am I going to eat over there?

Most universities require that first-year students buy a meal plan. This is because first-year students must live in dorms and not all dorms have kitchen facilities. A meal plan allows students to eat at the dining halls. You are given a set number of meals a week, and some meal plans include extra dollars that you can use to buy food from the school's food court. Once students start living in apartments or off-campus, they may decide to buy a smaller meal plan that allows them to eat lunch on campus each day, and then have dinner at home. Eating out is also quite popular, particularly among students who do not know how to cook!

到國外後，該如何解決吃的問題？

大部分的大學規定一年級生必須在學校餐廳搭伙，因為一年級生必須住宿舍，而宿舍裡面不一定有廚房設備。參加搭伙的學生可以在學校餐廳裡用餐；每個禮拜會有固定的用餐次數，有的搭伙方案還包括一些額外的錢，可以讓你在學校餐飲中心買食物。在學生住進公寓或搬出校外之後，可以考慮參加較小型的搭伙方案，每天在學校吃午餐，晚餐則回家吃。外食也很普通，不會作菜的學生尤其喜歡！

Top 10 必會字彙

★ **breakfast place**   *n.* 早餐店
[ˈbrɛkfəst ˌples]

★ **brunch**   *n.* 早午餐
[brʌntʃ]

★ **two-for-one**   *n.* 二人同行一人免費
[ˌtu fɔr ˈwʌn]

★ **bagger**   *n.* 裝袋員
[ˈbægɚ]

★ **deli section**   *n.* 熟食區
[ˈdɛlɪ ˌsɛkʃən]

★ **co-op**   *n.* 合作社
[ˈkoˌɑp]

★ **in bulk**   *adv.* 大包裝地；整批地
[ɪn ˈbʌlk]

★ **organic produce**   *n.* 有機蔬果
[ɔrˈgænɪk ˈprodjus]

★ **dining commons**   *n.* （大學等的）餐廳
[ˈdaɪnɪŋ ˌkɑməns]

★ **food court**   *n.* 餐飲中心；美食街
[ˈfud ˌkort]

CD **1-31**

1 A: Let's go to that breakfast place for brunch this Sunday.

B: Sounds good. They have a nice two-for-one.

A: 這個禮拜天我們去那間早餐店吃早午餐吧。

B: 好主意。那家店有二人同行一人免費，還不賴。

---

2 A: I was a bagger in a grocery store last summer.

B: Really? Me too. I also worked in the deli section.

A: 我去年夏天在一家雜貨店當裝袋員。

B: 真的嗎？我也是。我也在熟食區工作。

---

3 A: I like buying things at the co-op. They sell a lot in bulk.

B: And they've got great organic produce.

A: 我喜歡到合作社買東西。那兒很多東西都是量販的。

B: 而且那裡的有機蔬果很棒。

---

4 A: Wanna eat in the dining commons?

B: Nah. Let's eat at the food court instead.

A: 要不要去學校餐廳吃東西？

B: 不要。我們到美食街去吃吧。

你可以跟我這樣說

CD **1-32**

Dialogue A

Kevin goes to the supermarket with his friend.

Kevin: Okay, let's see. I need to get bread, milk, laundry detergent ...

Brian: And chips, soda, beer, and pretzels! Tonight's football game is gonna be awesome.

Kevin: How many guys are coming over to watch the game tonight?

Brian: I dunno. Probably eight? We'll need to order pizzas, too.

Kevin: Where are the pretzels?

Brian: Probably where the chips are. And don't forget the dip!

Kevin: Okay, you head over there. I need to pick up some ketchup. Meet you at the cashiers.

Kevin finds a supermarket employee.

Kevin: Excuse me, where can I find the ketchup?

Employee: In aisle 3, towards the back on the right side. You'll find all the condiments in that aisle.

Kevin: Thanks.

Kevin buys his groceries and meets Brian by the cashiers.

Check-out clerk: Paper or plastic?

Kevin: Plastic.

Check-out clerk: That'll be $52.76, sir. *(Kevin takes out his check card.)* Credit or debit?

Kevin: Debit, please.

Kevin swipes his card through the card reader and punches in his PIN.

Check-out clerk: Cash back?

Kevin: No, thank you.

Check-out clerk: Here's your receipt. Have a good day!

凱文和朋友上超市。

凱文： 好，我看看。我得買麵包、牛奶、洗衣精……

布萊恩： 還有洋芋片、汽水、啤酒跟麻花鹹餅乾！今天晚上的足球賽一定會很精彩。

凱文： 晚上有幾個人要來看球賽？

布萊恩： 不知，大概會有八個人吧。我們還得訂披薩。

凱文： 麻花餅乾在哪裡？

布萊恩： 應該和洋芋片放在同一個地方。別忘了買沾醬！

凱文： 好，你到那裡找，我得去買蕃茄醬。待會在收銀台見。

凱文找了一位超市員工。

凱文： 對不起，請問蕃茄醬放在哪裡？

*超市員工：*在第三走道，靠右後方。所有的佐料都在那個走道上。

凱文： 謝謝。

凱文採購完，和布萊恩在收銀台碰面。

收銀員： 紙袋還是塑膠袋？

凱文： 塑膠袋。

收銀員： 總共 **52.76** 美元，先生。*（凱文拿出他的支票卡。）*簽帳或直接扣款？

凱文： 直接扣款，麻煩你。

凱文用支票卡刷了讀卡機，然後鍵入密碼。

收銀員： 要提領現金嗎？

凱文： 不用，謝謝。

收銀員： 您的收據。祝您有愉快的一天！

[Words & Phrases]

- laundry detergent [`lɔndrɪ dɪˌtɝˋʤənt] *n.* 洗衣粉；洗衣精
- pretzel [`prɛtsl̩] *n.* 一種鹹脆捲餅
- awesome [`ɔsəm] *adj.* (口語) 很棒的
- dip [dɪp] *n.* 沾醬
- condiment [`kɑndəmənt] *n.* 佐料；調味料
- Paper or plastic [`plæstɪk]? 紙袋或塑膠袋？
- Credit or debit [`dɛbɪt]? 簽帳或直接扣款？
- swipe [swaɪp] *v.* 刷 (卡)
- punch in 打入；鍵入
- cash back 此指用支票卡提領現金
- receipt [rɪ`sit] *n.* 收據

你可以跟我這樣說

 CD **1-33**

Dialogue B

Annie and Liz are having dinner in the dining hall.

Annie: The dining hall is always so crowded. Quick, grab a tray before they run out.

Liz: What do you feel like eating?

Annie: I don't know. I'm kind of sick of the dining hall food. We eat the same stuff day in day out. I think I'll hit the salad bar first.

Liz: I'm going over to the pasta station. I'll meet you by the soda fountains. I hope we can find a table.

Annie and Liz get their food and meet up by the drink machines.

Liz: The pasta server was so rude! I asked if the sauce was vegetarian and she was like, "How should I know? Who cares?"

Annie: That sucks. Do you see an empty table?

Liz: There's one by the window.

Annie and Liz sit down.

Liz: What dressing is that?

Annie: Ranch, but it's fat-free. I hate fat-free dressing. It doesn't taste as good as normal dressing, but it was all they had left.

Liz: This pasta is overcooked. I think the sauce does have meat in it. Great, what am I supposed to eat now?

Annie: There are always the cereal bins.

Liz: I love cereal, but even I'm getting sick of eating it for breakfast, lunch, and dinner.

Annie: You know, I think the only good thing about the dining hall is the make-your-own waffle stations they have in the morning. Oh, and the sundaes!

Liz: Great. Pasta, cereal, waffles, and sundaes. There's no way I'm escaping the Freshman Fifteen.

安妮和莉姿在學校餐廳裡吃晚餐。

安妮：學校餐廳裡每次人都好多。快，趁餐盤還沒被拿光前，趕快拿一個。
莉姿：妳想吃什麼？
安妮：不知道。我有一點吃厭學校餐廳的食物了。我們每天都吃同樣的東西。我想先去沙拉吧。
莉姿：我要去義大利麵攤。等一下和妳在冷飲部見。希望能找得到空桌。

安妮和莉姿各自拿了食物後，在飲料機前碰面。

莉姿：義大利麵攤的服務員態度好差！我問她醬汁是不是素的，她竟然一付「我怎麼知道？管它的！」的態度。
安妮：有夠差勁。有沒有看到空桌？
莉姿：窗子那邊有一張。

安妮和莉姿坐下來。

莉姿：那是哪一種沙拉醬？
安妮：田園沙拉醬，但是是無脂的。我討厭無脂沙拉醬，沒有一般的醬好吃，但也只剩這種的了。
莉姿：這義大利麵煮過頭了。這個醬裡面真的有肉。這下可好了，現在我要怎麼吃？
安妮：總還有穀類攤囉。
莉姿：我是愛吃穀類食品，不過早餐、午餐還有晚餐都吃，我都快吐了。
安妮：妳知道嗎！我覺得學校餐廳唯一可取的是早上的「自己做鬆餅」攤。哦，還有聖代！
莉姿：太好了。義大利麵、穀類食品、鬆餅、聖代。我絕對逃不了「新鮮人十五磅」的命運了。

[Words & Phrases]

- grab [græb] *v.* 抓住；搶佔
- day in day out 天天
- hit [hɪt] *v.* （口語）到達；抵達
- soda fountain [ˈsodə ˌfauntn̩] *n.* 冷飲販賣部
- rude [rud] *adj.* 粗魯的；不禮貌的
- vegetarian [ˌvɛdʒəˈtɛrɪən] *adj.* 素的
- That sucks. 有夠差、爛、嘔。
- dressing [ˈdrɛsɪŋ] *n.* 沙拉醬

- ranch [rænʧ] *n.* 田園沙拉醬
- fat-free [ˈfæt ˈfri] *adj.* 無脂的
- overcooked [ˌovəˈkukt] *adj.* 煮太久的
- cereal bins [ˈsɪrɪəl ˌbɪnz] *n.* 穀類食品攤
- waffle [ˈwɑfl] *n.* 蛋奶鬆餅
- sundae [ˈsʌnde] *n.* 聖代
- Freshman Fifteen 指大學新鮮人因飲食習慣改變體重增加 15 磅的現象

留學 超實用單字

CD 1-34

Going Out to Eat 外食

★ host / hostess [host] / [ˋhostɪs] *n.* 男／女招待員

You: How long do we have to wait for a table?
Friend: The hostess said it would probably be 20 minutes.

你： 我們要等多久才會有空桌？
朋友： 女招待員說大概要 20 分鐘。

★ pager [ˋpedʒɚ] *n.* 傳呼器

You: We'd like a table for three, please.
Host: It's going to be at least a half an hour wait. I'll give you a pager so you can walk around. When a table opens up, we'll page you.

你： 我們要一張三人桌，麻煩你。
招待員： 您至少得等半小時。我給您一個傳呼器，你們可以在附近逛一逛。一有空桌，我們會呼叫您。

★ special [ˋspɛʃəl] *n.* 特餐

You: Excuse me, what are today's specials?
Waiter: Today we have baked pasta in a meat sauce and roast¹ chicken with baked potato.

你： 對不起，請問今日特餐是什麼？
服務生： 我們今天有焗烤肉醬義大利麵，和烤雞佐烤洋芋。

[Word List]

1. roast [rost] *adj.* 烤過的

★ **substitution** [ˌsʌbstə`tjuʃən] *n.* **替換**

You: Can I please have my salad with no tomatoes or onions?
Waiter: I'm sorry. We don't allow substitutions.

你： 我的沙拉可不可以不要放蕃茄和洋蔥？
服務生：抱歉，沒辦法替換。

★ **allergic** [ə`lɜˊdʒɪk] *adj.* **過敏的**

You: Is it possible to have the pasta without shrimp?[1] I'm allergic to shrimp.
Waiter: No problem. Would you like salmon[2] instead?

你： 義大利麵裡面可不可以不要放蝦子？我對蝦過敏。
服務生：沒問題。那要不要換成鮭魚呢？

★ **refill** [`ri͵fɪl] *n.* **續杯**

You: Excuse me, are there refills on drinks?
Waiter: Yes, we give refills for all fountain drinks and iced tea.

你： 對不起，請問飲料可不可以續杯？
服務生：可以，所有的汽水和冰紅茶都可以續杯。

[**Word List**]

1. shrimp [ʃrɪmp] *n.* 小蝦　　　　2. salmon [`sæmən] *n.* 鮭魚

CD 1-35

★ buffet [bə`fe] *n.* 自助餐

You: Does that restaurant have a buffet?
Friend: Yes! It's all-you-can-eat for just $12.99.

你： 那家餐廳有沒有自助餐？
朋友： 有！吃到飽的只要 12.99 美元。

★ rare / medium / well-done [rɛr] / [`midɪəm] / [`wɛl`dʌn]
adj. 三分熟 / 五分熟 / 全熟

Waiter: How would you like your steak? Rare, medium, or well-done?
You: Medium, please.

服務生： 請問您的牛排要幾分熟？三分熟、五分熟還是全熟？
你： 五分熟，麻煩你。

★ takeout [`tek͵aut] *n.* 外帶；外賣

You: Do you want to order[1] pizza tonight?
Roommate: No. Let's order some Chinese takeout.

你： 今晚想不想訂披薩？
室友： 不要。我們叫中國菜外賣吧。

[Word List]

1. order [`ɔrdə] *v.* 訂購

⭐ delivery [dɪˋlɪvərɪ] *n.* 遞送

You *(on the phone)*: I'd like to order a pizza, please. For delivery.
Employee: Okay. What's your address?

你（電話線上）： 麻煩你，我想訂一個披薩。外送。
員工： 好的。您的地址是？

⭐ stuffed [stʌft] *adj.* 吃得很飽的

Waiter: Would you two like dessert?[1]
You: No thanks. I'm stuffed!

服務生： 請問兩位要不要點甜點？
你： 不要了，謝謝。我好飽！

[**Word List**]

1. dessert [dɪˋzɝt] *n.* 餐後的甜點

留學 佈告欄

Shopping List

- ramen[1] (chicken/beef)
- potato chips
- soda
- milk
- cereal
- pop tarts[2]
- coffee

- tea bags
- ice cream
- cookies
- string cheese[3]
- crackers[4]
- popcorn

[翻 譯]

購物清單

- 拉麵（雞肉 / 牛肉）
- 洋芋片
- 汽水
- 牛奶
- 穀類食品
- 水果餡餅
- 咖啡

- 茶包
- 冰淇淋
- 餅乾
- 乳酪條
- 蘇打餅乾
- 爆米花

[Word List]

1. ramen [`rɑmɛn] *n.* 拉麵
2. pop tart [`pɑp ˌtɑrt] *n.* 水果餡餅
3. string cheese [`strɪŋ ˌtʃiz] *n.* 乳酪條
4. cracker [`krækɚ] *n.* 蘇打餅乾

留學 智慧王

What is Cash Back? 什麼是現金提領？

在美國的 Wal-Mart、Kmart、Target 等商店、超市和藥局都有現金提領的服務；你可以用支票卡提領現金。在超市用支票卡付帳時，收銀員會問你要不要順便提領現金。如果你要，讀卡機會問你要領多少現金，只要選擇好金額，收銀員便會把現金和收據一併給你。消費金額和所提領之金額便會從你的銀行帳戶中扣除。

購物時順便提領現金在美國很普遍，因為有時很難找到提款機。記得，如果使用的是其他銀行的提款機，該銀行和你的銀行會分別向你收取手續費。如果是購物時順便提領現金，則不需付手續費，因此很多人覺得這種提款方式非常方便。

Freshman Fifteen 新鮮人十五磅

新鮮人 15 磅指的是大一新鮮人若不注意自己的飲食，便可能增加的體重數（15 磅 /6.8 公斤！）。許多學生不住家裡後，常會吃不健康的食物，如洋芋片、冰淇淋、披薩、糖果等，尤其是在晚上讀書的時候，更是容易吃進這些垃圾食物。當生活忙碌，飲食不正常時，大一生一不小心就會發胖。如要避免「新鮮人十五磅」的命運，應該經常做運動（連走路上學都有助益），務必每天按時吃三餐，不要餐餐吃披薩！

American Portions 美式份量

美國餐廳最有名的是什麼？就是菜的份量！上館子時，看到服務生端來比你想像還多得多的一大盤菜時，請別感到意外。份量大正是很多美國人過胖的一個原因；份量大會讓你在不知不覺中吃得比在家裡時還多。美國人喜歡物超所值，但你也不需硬撐吃完所有的菜。能吃多少就吃多少，吃不完的剩菜可以請服務生打包帶回家。

Tipping Etiquette 給小費的成規

　　與其他收取服務費的國家不同，在美國給小費是很普遍的作法。如果服務周到，習慣上應該至少給 15% 的小費，但如果非常滿意，多給一點也無妨。美國人大多會把錢放在桌上（包括餐飲費和小費）；如果要在收銀台付錢，小費可以留在桌上。

A Taste of Home 家鄉的味道

　　對許多外籍學生來說，最難的事情莫過於找家鄉口味的食物。你若不是在紐約、洛杉磯或舊金山等地留學，在美國很難找到好吃的中國餐館。大學城中的中國餐館多半是外帶式，而且做的是美式中國菜。有的學生會自己做菜，但除非你住公寓，或者宿舍裡有公用廚房，否則不大可能在家做飯。中國料理的基本食材大多在當地的超市就買得到；如果要買很少見的食材，通常到美食或國際雜貨店就找得到。有的城市還有亞洲雜貨店，從水餃皮到麻薯冰淇淋應有盡有。如果你是在西岸，99 Ranch Market（大華超級市場）裡什麼都買得到。

Eating and Food-related Terms 飲食與食物相關用語 CD 1-36

• anorexia [ˌænəˈrɛksɪə]	*n.* 厭食症
• eating disorder [ˈitɪŋ ˌdɪsˈɔrdə]	*n.* 飲食失調症
• binge-purge syndrome [ˈbɪndʒˈpɝdʒ ˌsɪndrom]	*n.* 暴食症
• bulimia [buˈlɪmɪə]	*n.* 暴食症
• vegan [ˈvigən]	*n.* 嚴守素食主義的人
• vegetarian [ˌvɛdʒəˈtɛrɪən]	*n.* 素食主義者
• low-cholesterol [ˈlo kəˈlɛstəˌrol]	*adj.* 低膽固醇的
• non-fat [ˈnɑnˈfæt]	*adj.* 脫脂的
• anti-oxidant [ˌæntaɪˈɑksədənt]	*n.* 抗氧化物
• non-dairy [ˈnɑnˈdɛrɪ]	*adj.* 不含乳製品的

chapter 6

Chapter 6

Cars and Transportation

汽車和交通問題

How do I get around?

Many students ask if they will need a car in the U.S. In some cases, a car is necessary. Having a car can make your life more convenient, but if you go to school in a big city, it probably isn't necessary. Many schools have their own bus systems, and most places will be within walking distance. Spend at least a semester without a car to see if you really need one. Otherwise, having a bicycle is an option, and many students opt to walk everywhere.

我該怎麼解決交通問題？

很多學生會問，在美國需不需要買車。在某些情況下，車子確實有必要。有車會讓你的生活比較方便，但是如果在大城市唸書，可能就沒有此一必要了。很多學校有自己的公車系統，而大部分的地方也都在步行距離以內。至少先過一學期沒有車的生活，再決定是否真的需要一部車。不然的話，買輛腳踏車是另一種選擇，而很多學生則選擇走路。

Top 10 必會字彙

CD **1-37**

★ **stick shift**
['stɪk ˌʃɪft]
n. 手排檔

★ **expire**
[ɪk`spaɪr]
v. 過期

★ **renew**
[rɪ`nu]
v. 更新

★ **learner's permit**
['lɜnəz ˌpɝmɪt]
n. 學習駕照

★ **road test**
['rod ˌtɛst]
n. 路考

★ **organ donor**
['ɔrgən ˌdonə]
n. 器官捐贈者

★ **handbook**
['hænd,bʊk]
n. 手冊

★ **walking distance**
['wɔkɪŋ ˌdɪstəns]
n. 步行距離

★ **bus route**
['bʌs ˌrut]
n. 公車路線圖

★ **parking permit**
['parkɪŋ ˌpɝmɪt]
n. 停車證

1 A: Hey, do you know how to drive a stick shift?

B: No. Besides, I can't drive right now. My license expired and I haven't renewed it.

A: 嘿，你會不會開手排車？

B: 不會。而且我現在沒辦法開車。我的駕照過期了，還沒去更新。

2 A: If I get a learner's permit, do I have to take a road test?

B: Yep. And you need to decide about being an organ donor. Check the handbook.

A: 如果我拿到學習駕照，還需要考路考嗎？

B: 是的。你還得決定是否要當器官捐贈者。請看一看手冊。

3 A: Is the library within walking distance from here?

B: No, it's pretty far. You can take a bus. I'll show you the bus route.

A: 從這裡去圖書館是不是在步行距離以內？

B: 不，圖書館滿遠的。你可以搭公車，我來跟你講公車的路線。

4 A: I'm getting tired of walking to class.

B: I'll give you a ride. I have a parking permit this semester.

A: 我厭倦了走路去上課。

B: 我載你去。我這學期拿到了一張停車證。

你可以跟我這樣說

CD **1-39**

Dialogue A

*Kevin goes to the DMV to get a driver's license. He steps up to the **counter** when his number is called.*

Kevin: Hi, I'd like to apply for a driver's license.

DMV Clerk: Did you fill out the necessary application?

Kevin: Yes, and I brought my passport and Taiwanese driver's license. I also have my social security card.

DMV Clerk: All right. You'll first need to take a vision test. Please look into the viewer and read the letters off. Start at the top and read left to right. After you finish each line, move on to the next.

Kevin: Okay ... A, J, I, P ... n, e, w, v ... B, M, um ... H ... L ...

DMV Clerk: That's fine. Now you need to take the traffic laws and signs test. Please go over to the computer. Take as much time as you need. Your answers will be corrected immediately.

Kevin takes the test and comes back.

Kevin: I passed!

DMV Clerk: Right. I'll need your thumbprint. Please place your right thumb on this inkpad and place your thumb in this box *(pointing to a section on the form)*. Since your current license is from another country, you'll have to make an appointment for a driving test. How's tomorrow at 11 a.m.?

Kevin: Sure. Will I need to bring anything?

DMV Clerk: Nope. We'll see you tomorrow.

凱文到監理所申請駕照。叫到他的號碼時，他走到櫃台前。

凱文： 你好，我想申請汽車駕照。

監理所辦事員：必要的申請表都填好了嗎？

凱文： 填好了，我帶了護照和台灣的駕照，還帶了社會安全卡。

監理所辦事員：好。你需要先做一下視力測驗。請看幻燈機，把上面的字母唸出來。從上面開始，由左唸到右。唸完一行後，就接著唸下一行。

凱文： 好……A、J、I、P…n、e、w、v…B、M，呃……H…L…

監理所辦事員：可以了。現在你得考交通規則和號誌測驗。請到電腦那邊，不限時間作答。你的答案會馬上改好。

凱文考了測驗，然後回來。

凱文： 我過了！

監理所辦事員：好的。我需要你的拇指印。請用右手拇指按一下印泥，然後把指印印在這個格子裡 *(指向申請表某處)*。由於你目前的駕照非本國駕照，你需要預約時間考路考。明天早上 11 點可以嗎？

凱文： 行。我需要帶什麼東西嗎？

監理所辦事員：不用。明天見。

[Words & Phrases]

- DMV (=Department of Motor Vehicles) 監理所
- counter [`kaʊntɚ] *n.* 櫃台
- application [ˌæpləˋkeʃən] *n.* 申請（書、表）
- vision test [ˋvɪʒən ˌtɛst] *n.* 視力測驗
- viewer [ˋvjuɚ] *n.* 幻燈機
- read off 按順序唸出來
- thumbprint [ˋθʌmˌprɪnt] *n.* 拇指印（紋）
- inkpad [ˋɪŋkˌpæd] *n.* 印泥
- box [bɑks] *n.* （報紙等的）方塊；（表格等的）格子

你可以跟我這樣說

Dialogue B

Annie is studying in the library with her friend Tyler.

Annie: It's already midnight? I've been studying for six hours straight! I'm going home. Are you staying here?

Tyler: Maybe. I still have a couple of chapters to read. How are you getting home?

Annie: I'll just walk. The buses aren't running and my dorm is just a 15-minute walk away.

Tyler: You can't walk by yourself at night. It's dangerous. I'll walk you back.

Annie: No, it's okay. Besides, when I'm in Taiwan, I walk around at night all the time.

Tyler: Yeah, but that's Taiwan. Here you have to be careful, even in a college town like this one. Why do you think we have the blue-light phones all over the place? Plus, some of the paths and sidewalks aren't very well lit. It's always best to walk with someone.

Annie: But you still have some studying to do. Oh, I know! There's my friend Alex. Maybe he drove to the library. If he did, I'll see if he can give me a ride back to the dorms.

Tyler: All right, but if he can't, come back here and we'll walk back to our dorms together.

Annie: OK. Thanks Tyler!

Tyler: It's no problem. Besides, I'm starting to get pretty tired. A walk is just what I need to wake up a bit and finish my reading.

安妮和朋友泰勒在圖書館唸書。

安妮：已經半夜了？我已經連續唸了六小時的書！我要回家了。你還要留下來嗎？

泰勒：可能吧。我還有兩三章要看。妳要怎麼回家？

安妮：就走路吧。公車已經停駛了，而我的宿舍只要走 15 分鐘就到了。

泰勒：晚上不要一個人走路，很危險。我陪妳走回去。

安妮：不用，沒關係。再說我在台灣的時候，經常一個人晚上到處亂走。

泰勒：是啊，但那是在台灣。在這裡妳得小心，就算在這種大學城也一樣。不然妳想我們為什麼到處都設有緊急電話？況且，有的小路和人行道的燈光很暗，最好還是有人跟妳一起走。

安妮：可是你還有書要看。哦，有了！我的朋友艾力克斯，或許他是開車來圖書館的。如果是的話，我去問他可不可以載我一程回宿舍。

泰勒：好吧，但是如果他不行的話，回來這裡，我們再一起走回宿舍。

安妮：好。謝啦，泰勒！

泰勒：不成問題。況且我也開始覺得挺累的。我現在正需要出去走走，清醒一下好把書唸完。

[Words & Phrases]

- straight [stret] *adv.* 連續地；不間斷地
- run [rʌn] *v.*（交通工具）行駛；通行
- college town [`kɑlɪdʒ `taun] *n.* 大學城
- blue-light phone [`blu`laɪt ˌfon] *n.* 緊急電話（或稱為 emergency phone）
- path [pæθ] *n.* 小徑；窄路
- sidewalk [`saɪdˌwɔk] *n.* 人行道
- give sb. a ride 載某人一程

留學　超實用單字

CD **1-41**

At the DMV 在監理所

★ valid [ˈvælɪd] *adj.* 有效的

You:　Can I drive if I only have an international driver's license?
Clerk:　I'm sorry. An international driver's license is not a valid license. You must have an actual license from your home country.

你：　　如果我只有國際駕照，可以開車嗎？
辦事員：很抱歉，國際駕照不是有效的駕照。你必須持有您的國家的真正駕照。

★ replace [rɪˈples] *v.* 補發；替換

You:　How much will it cost to replace my driver's license?
Clerk:　A replacement license costs $10.

你：　　請問補發駕照要多少錢？
辦事員：補發駕照要 10 美元。

★ register [ˈrɛgɪstɚ] *v.* 登記；註冊

You:　Hello. I'd like to register my car.
Clerk:　All right. I'll need the bill of sale[1] for the car, and I need to see your ID.

你：　　你好。我想登記我的車子。
辦事員：好的，我需要車子的買賣證明，還要看一下你的身份證。

[Word List]

1. bill of sale 賣據

★ parallel park [ˋpærəˌlɛl ˋpɑrk] *v.* 平行停車

You: Will I have to drive on the freeway[1] during the driving test?

Clerk: You might. And you will definitely have to parallel park. Make sure you can do that before the exam.

你：   路考的時候我得開上高速公路嗎？

辦事員：可能需要。而且你一定要會平行停車。考前務必要學會。

★ driver handbook [ˋdraɪvɚ ˌhændbʊk] *n.* 駕駛手冊

You: Where can I get a copy of the driver handbook?

Clerk: They're on that rack over there. You can also download one from our website.

你：   我在哪兒能拿到一份駕駛手冊？

辦事員：那邊的架子上有。你也可以從網站上下載。

Other Transportation 其他交通工具

★ automatic [ˌɔtəˋmætɪk] *n.* 自動排檔汽車；自動變速器

You: Is your car an automatic or a manual?[2]

Roommate: Automatic. I can't drive a stick shift. Hey, need a lift[3] to class?

你：   你的車是自排車還是手排車？

室友： 自排車。我不會開手排車。嘿，要搭便車去上課嗎？

[Word List]

1. freeway [ˋfriˌwe] *n.* （通常不收費的）高速公路

2. manual [ˋmænjʊəl] *n.* 手排車

3. lift [lɪft] *n.* 便車

CD 1-42

★ bike rack [`baɪk ˌræk] *n.* 腳踏車停放架

You: Did you walk to class?
Friend: No, I rode my bike. I left it at the bike rack near the bus
            stop.

你：   你是走路來上課的嗎？
朋友：   沒有，我騎腳踏車。我把腳踏車停在公車站附近的腳踏車停放
            架。

★ subway [`sʌbˌwe] *n.* 地下鐵

You: You live off campus, right? Do you drive your own car to
            school?
Friend: No, I take the subway to Telegraph[1] Ave.,[2] and then ride
            the bus from there.

你：   你住校外，對不對？你自己開車上學嗎？
朋友：   不，我搭地鐵到電報大道站，然後在那邊搭公車。

★ commuter train [kə`mjutɚ ˌtren] *n.* 通勤列車

Friend: I want to visit my friend in Boston this weekend, but I can't
            find anyone to give me a ride.
You: Take the commuter train. It's not expensive, and you won't
            get stuck[3] in all the traffic.

朋友：   我這週末想去波士頓拜訪朋友，但找不到人可以載我一程。
你：   搭通勤列車吧。票價不貴，而且一路上也不會塞車。

[Word List]

1. telegraph [`tɛləˌgræf] *n.* 電報（機）

2. Ave. (=avenue [`ævəˌnju]) *n.* 大街；
   大道

3. get stuck 動彈不得

⑤ campus shuttle [ˌkæmpəs ˋʃʌtl̩] *n.* 校園接駁車

Friend: How did you get from the parking lot to the library?

You: I took the campus shuttle. I think it was the red line.

朋友：　你們怎麼從停車場到圖書館？

你：　　我搭校園接駁車。我想應該是紅線。

⑥ SUV [ˋes ˋju ˋvi] *n.* 運動休旅車

You： That big car over there is an SUV, right? What's that stand for?

Friend：It stands for sport-utility[1] vehicle.[2]

你：　　那邊那輛大車是台 SUV，對吧？那是什麼意思？

朋友：　意思是運動休旅車。

[Word List]

1. utility [juˋtɪlətɪ] *n.* 效用；實用

2. vehicle [ˋviɪkl̩] *n.* 車輛；交通工具

佈告欄

CALIFORNIA
DRIVER LICENSE
N4062778

CLASS:C

EXPIRES 08-01-2009

JONATHAN CHARLES SHAW
167 POPPY ST
LA MESA CA 13567

SEX:M   HAIR:BRN   EYES:BRN
HT:6-02   WT:170   DOB:04-01-1980

05/01/2000 235 RB FD/07

[翻 譯]

加州監理所
駕照

過期日 08-01-2009   N4062778   等級：C

強納森‧查爾斯‧蕭
13567 加州拉梅莎
派比街 167 號

性別：男   髮色：棕色   眼睛顏色：棕色
身高：6 呎 2 吋   體重：170 磅   出生日期：04-01-1980

留學 智慧王

Do I Really Need a Car? 我真的需要一部車嗎？

雖然大部分的學生覺得車子並非必需品，不過如果你的學校和住處不在同一地區，開車可能會比較方便。有的大學甚至不允許一年級生開車進校園。這麼做除了可以減少車流量外，也可以給一年級生一個機會能定下心來好好地探索學校環境。如果你覺得自己很忙，有車會讓你的生活方便些，那麼可以考慮購買二手車。不過請記住，學校附近的停車位總是有限，搭公車甚至走路或許還比較方便。

How to Get a Driver's License? 如何申請駕照？

每州申請駕照的規定不同。以加州為例，外籍學生不需要申請加州駕照，只要持有自己國家的有效駕照即可。國際駕照並不被認為是有效的駕照。在其他州，如果你有工作，則可能會被要求申請一張當地的駕照。

你可以在 www.dmv.org 網站查詢各州的規定。這個網站提供各州監理所的資訊，請仔細閱讀申請程序。有些地方的監理分所會建議你先預約，以免大排長龍。如果規定要考筆試，務必閱讀該州的監理所手冊（DMV handbook），或先做幾次模擬測驗。

What About a Bike? Or a Scooter? 那腳踏車呢？機車又如何？

如果上下課的路途較遠，又不想花力氣找車位，腳踏車是很好用的交通工具。但是，請留意當地的天氣狀況。當外面冷得要命的時候，你應該不會想騎著腳踏車到處跑吧！速克達機車（scooters，或稱 mopeds）在美國不是很普遍。較重型的機車在美國較容易買得到，但不是每所學校的校園都適合騎。再次提醒，如果就讀的學校地處冬季嚴寒的地方，機車就不是很實用了。

Safety 安全

大部分的學校很重視安全。在台灣,夜深時在鬧區還常會看到有人走動,但在美國請小心一點。以下為一般注意事項:

★ 不要一個人走夜路。

★ 如果必須在晚上走路回家,至少跟一名友人一起走。

★ 永遠走在燈光明亮的地帶。

★ 善用學校提供的服務。比方說,有些學校有夜間小型公車服務,在一般公車停駛後發車。

★ 善用常識和直覺。如果感覺到有危險,趕快找緊急電話,或者到離你最近、有人走動的明亮地帶。

Getting Gas 加油

美國大部分的加油站都是自助式的(*self-serve*),意思就是你得自己加油。自助加油可以減低汽油的價錢,不過對從來沒有自己加過油的學生而言,可能是個讓人困惑的經驗!如果你不確定該怎麼做的話,第一次加油時可以帶個朋友一起去。大部分的加油站都接受支票卡,你可以在加油處直接付帳,不必進入加油站裡。

CD **1-43**

A Few More Words for the Road 上路前多知道幾個字吧

- carpool [`kɑr,pul]   v. 共乘
- skateboard [`sket,bord]   n. 滑板
- in-line skate [`ɪn,laɪn `sket]   n. 直排輪
- mountain bike [`maʊntn̩ ,baɪk]   n. 越野腳踏車
- folding bike [`foldɪŋ ,baɪk]   n. 折疊式腳踏車
- BMX bike [`bi`ɛm`ɛks ,baɪk]   n. 花式越野單車
- Razor scooter [`ræzɚ ,skutɚ]   n. 單腳踏板車
- pogo stick [`pogo ,stɪk]   n. 彈跳桿
- road bike [`rod ,baɪk]   n. 重型機車
- beach cruiser [`bitʃ ,kruzɚ]   n. 海灘車
- grandma bike [`grændmɑ ,baɪk]   n. 附籃子的腳踏車
- car insurance [`kɑr ɪn,ʃʊrəns]   n. 汽車保險
- oil change [`ɔil ,tʃendʒ]   n. 換機油
- tune-up [`tun,ʌp]   n. 汽車檢修
- parking ticket [`pɑrkɪŋ ,tɪkɪt]   n. 停車罰單
- parking meter [`pɑrkɪŋ ,mitɚ]   n. 停車收費器
- flat tire [,flæt `taɪr]   n. 輪胎沒氣；爆胎
- dead battery [`dɛd `bætərɪ]   n. 耗光電瓶

Chapter 7

Libraries 圖書館

Stacks? Like a stack of books?

University libraries are a completely different world. Endless shelves of books. The feeling that you're going to get lost if you venture too far into the back. The library is an important part of any student's university experience. Many students prefer to study in the library, and each library usually has its own "personality." Some, usually called "Stacks," are old-fashioned buildings with an incredible number of books and usually have a very quiet and studious atmosphere. Others allow talking, and are great venues for group or project work. No matter what you use the library for, you'll be spending a lot of time in there during your years of study. So, find your library, hunker down, and get to work!

書庫？你是指一大堆書嗎？

大學圖書館是個完全不同的世界，一排又一排無止境的書架，讓人有一種太深入就會出不來的感覺。圖書館在每個大學生求學時都扮演了很重要的角色。許多學生喜歡在圖書館唸書，每個圖書館也通常都有自己的「個性」。有些圖書館（通常稱作「書庫」）是傳統的建築物，裡面藏書量驚人，而且通常有一股極為安靜和用功的氣氛。其他圖書館則允許人們說話，是做分組功課或計畫的最佳場所。不管你上圖書館的目的是什麼，求學期間一定會經常泡在那裡。所以囉，趕快找到適合自己的圖書館，坐下來，好好用功吧！

Top 10 必會字彙

 CD **2-01**

★ **return** [rɪ`tɜ·n]	*v.* 還書
② ★ **late fee** [`let ˌfi]	*n.* 逾期罰款
③ ★ **due date** [`dju ˌdet]	*n.* 到期日
④ ★ **renew** [rɪ`nju]	*v.* 續借
⑤ ★ **drop-off slot** [`drɑp ˌɔf `slɑt]	*n.* 還書孔
⑥ ★ **on reserve** [ɑn rɪ`zɜ·v]	*adj.* 在預約保留架上
⑦ ★ **recall** [rɪ`kɔl]	*v.* 催還
⑧ ★ **exhibit** [ɪg`zɪbɪt]	*n.* 展覽
⑨ ★ **display** [dɪ`sple]	*n.* 展示
⑩ ★ **small group study room** [`smɔl `grup `stʌdɪ ˌrum]	*n.* 小團體閱讀室

CD 2-02

1 A: Hey, you had better return those books. Otherwise there will be a late fee.

B: Oh no! The due date was three days ago! How much am I going to have to pay?

A: 嘿，你最好趕快歸還那些書，否則會有逾期罰款。

B: 糟糕！還書日期是三天以前！我得付多少錢？

---

2 A: I've got to go to the library and renew some books.

B: While you're there, could you drop these books in the drop-off slot for me?

A: 我得去圖書館續借幾本書。

B: 去圖書館的時候，可不可以幫我把這幾本書投到還書孔裡？

---

3 A: The book I need is supposed to be on reserve, but it's not there. And it's not in the stacks either.

B: You can ask the library to recall it, but it might take a week or two to get it.

A: 我要的書應該在預約保留架上，可是並不在那兒，也不在書架上。

B: 你可以請圖書館催還，不過可能需要一兩個禮拜才拿得到。

---

4 A: You should check out the exhibit on Asian American Heritage.

B: I've heard they've got some great photographs on display. Where is it?

A: It's on the third floor, near the small group study rooms.

A: 你應該去看亞裔美人文物展。

B: 聽說他們展出的一些攝影作品很不錯。在哪裡展覽？

A: 在三樓，靠近小團體閱讀室。

你可以跟我這樣說

CD **2-03**

Dialogue A

Kevin goes to the library to do some research.

Kevin: Hi, I'm looking for books on electrical engineering.

Librarian: You'll need to search for relevant books. Go to one of the computers and search using our online catalog.

Kevin: How will I know where to find the books?

Librarian: Each book has a call number. Look at the letter at the beginning of the call number that will tell you which floor the book is on.

Kevin: Is there a directory I can look at?

Librarian: Sure. Just take this floor plan with you. If you have any problems, there's an assistant on each floor to help you.

Kevin: Thank you very much.

Kevin searches for his books and then goes to find them.

Ted: Hey Kevin, what are you doing here?

Kevin: I'm looking for a couple of books. Hey, do you know where the photocopiers are?

Ted: Each floor has a photocopier. There's one by the elevator on this floor.

Kevin: So are you always in the library?

Ted: Pretty much. I like studying here. Hardly anyone comes to this part of the stacks, so it's really quiet.

Kevin: I have a feeling I'm going to be spending a lot of time in here. This semester is going to be a lot of work!

凱文到圖書館找資料。

凱文：　　嗨，我想找電機工程的書。

圖書館員：你得先搜尋相關書籍。找台電腦，用我們的線上館藏目錄搜尋。

凱文：　　我要怎麼知道該到哪裡找書呢？

圖書館員：每本書都有一個編目號碼，看編目號碼開頭的字母，就知道那本書在哪一層樓了。

凱文：　　有沒有指南可以給我看？

圖書館員：當然有。你就帶著這張樓層圖，如果有任何問題，每層樓都有助理可以協助你。

凱文：　　非常謝謝你。

凱文搜尋完所需用書後便去找書。

泰德：　　嘿，凱文，你在這裡幹嘛？

凱文：　　我在找幾本書。嘿，你知不知道影印機在哪裡？

泰德：　　每層樓都有影印機。這樓的影印機在電梯旁邊。

凱文：　　那你常常待在圖書館囉？

泰德：　　幾乎吧。我喜歡在這裡唸書，書庫這邊很少人來，所以很安靜。

凱文：　　我有預感我得經常上圖書館來。這個學期的課業會很重！

[Words & Phrases]

- relevant [`rɛləvənt] *adj.* 相關的
- online catalog [`ɑn‚laɪn`kætl‚ɔg] *n.* 線上館藏目錄
- call number [`kɔl ‚nʌmbə] *n.*（書籍的）編目號碼
- directory [də`rɛktərɪ] *n.* 指南
- floor plan [`flɔr ‚plæn] *n.* 樓層圖
- photocopier [`fotə‚kɑpɪə] *n.* 影印機
- stacks [stæks] *n.*（圖書的）大型書架；書庫

你可以跟我這樣說

 CD 2-04

Dialogue B

Annie meets her classmates to work on a Psychology project.

Annie: Where should we sit? How about that big table by the window?

Peggy: Good idea. I'm going to get something from the vending machine. Want anything?

Annie: No, thanks. I'm going to check my e-mail while we wait for everyone else. Maybe I should check out a laptop as well.

Peggy: Good idea. That way, we can type up all of our ideas.

Annie goes to check out a laptop.

Annie: I love how there's wireless everywhere in the university. These laptops are great because then I don't have to lug around my own.

Peggy: I'm glad we're meeting at this library. I'll just stick around after we're done and do some studying.

Annie: How do you get any work done here? This library isn't quiet at all! No wonder they call it the "social library"!

Peggy: I can study here. I actually prefer a little bit of noise while I work. Plus, I like taking breaks and having people to talk to. If I really need to concentrate, I just go down to one of the silent floors.

Annie: I can't study here because I'm always tempted to go down to the Media Center. They have almost every movie ever made. It's so easy to borrow a DVD and watch it at one of the viewing stations.

Peggy: No wonder you always want our group to meet here!

安妮和同學碰面一起做心理學的大型作業。

安妮：我們要坐哪兒？窗戶旁邊那張大桌子怎麼樣？

珮姬：好主意，我要去販賣機買一點東西。妳有沒有想要買什麼？

安妮：不了，謝謝。我想趁等其他人的時候，去收一下電子郵件。或許我還該
　　　借一台筆記型電腦出來。

珮姬：好主意，這樣我們就可以把我們的想法全部打上去。

安妮去借筆記型電腦。

安妮：學校裡面到處都可以無線上網，真棒。這些筆記型電腦很不錯，這樣我
　　　就不必帶著自己的到處跑。

珮姬：我很高興我們約在這間圖書館。等我們討論完了之後，我要留下來唸
　　　書。

安妮：在這裡要怎麼做功課？這間圖書館一點也不安靜！難怪大家都叫它「社
　　　交圖書館」！

珮姬：我在這裡唸得下書。唸書的時候，我其實比較喜歡有一點聲音。而且我
　　　喜歡休息，也喜歡有人可以聊天。如果我真的需要專心，就下樓到禁音
　　　樓層去。

安妮：在這裡我沒辦法看書，因為每次都禁不住誘惑，想下樓到媒體中心去。
　　　幾乎所有出品過的電影他們都有。借片 DVD 到觀賞處看好簡單喔。

珮姬：難怪妳總要和我們的小組約在這裡！

[Words & Phrases]

- vending machine [ˋvɛndɪŋ məˏʃin] n.
  自動販賣機
- check out [ˋtʃɛk ˏaʊt] 借出（書等）
- laptop [ˋlæpˏtɑp] n. 手提電腦
- lug [lʌg] v. 使勁拉……；用力拖……
- stick around （在同一個地方）逗留；等待
- silent floor [ˋsaɪlənt ˏflɔr] n. 禁音樓層
- Media Center [ˋmidɪə ˏsɛntɚ] n. 媒體
  中心
- viewing station [ˋvjuɪŋ ˏsteʃən] n. 觀賞
  處

留學　超實用字彙

CD 2-05

The "Serious" Library「嚴肅」的圖書館

★ collection [kə`lɛkʃən] *n.* 館藏

You: I've heard that the library has a special collection of rare[1] books.

Friend: That's right. It contains original copies of all the famous works.

你： 我聽說這間圖書館有罕見書籍的特別館藏。

朋友： 沒錯，其中包含了許多原版的名著。

② cart [kɑrt] *n.* 小型推車

You: I've found all the books I'm looking for, but I don't think I need this one anymore.

Friend: Just put it on the cart next to the elevator, and the librarian will put it back on the shelf.

你： 我要找的書都找到了，但是這本好像已經不需要了。

朋友： 把它放到電梯旁邊的推車上就可以了，圖書館員會把它放回書架上。

③ circulation desk [ˌsɝkjə`leʃən ˌdɛsk] *n.* 借還書櫃台

You: Where do I return my books?

Friend: You can just leave them on the circulation desk. The drop-off counter is right next to where you check out books.

你： 我該到哪裏還書？

朋友： 把它們放在借還書櫃台上就可以了。還書櫃台就在你借書的地方旁邊。

[Word List]

1. rare [rɛr] *adj.* 罕見的

The "Social" Library 「社交」圖書館

★ projection room [prə`dʒɛkʃən ˌrum] *n.* 投影機室

You: The film club wants to show the newest Stephen Chow movie.
Friend: You should try to get a projection room in the library.

你： 電影社想放周星馳最新的電影。
朋友： 那你應該去圖書館借間投影室。

★ slide projector [`slaɪd prə¸dʒɛktə˞] *n.* 幻燈片投影機

Friend: Do you know where I can borrow a slide projector?
You: I'm not sure. My professor uses one for my art history class.
I'll ask if it's possible to borrow it.

朋友： 你知不知道哪裡可以借到幻燈片投影機？
你： 我不確定。我的教授上藝術史的時候會用。我去問問有沒有可能借到。

★ multi-format VCR [ˌmʌltar`fɔrmæt `vi `si `ar] *n.* 多規格錄放影機

You: Is this tape NTSC[1] or PAL?[2]
Friend: I'm not sure. You can watch it at the library because they have multi-format VCRs.

你： 這卷錄影帶是 NTSC 還是 PAL？
朋友： 我不確定。你可以在圖書館看，因為圖書館有多規格錄放影機。

[Word List]

1. NTSC (=National Television System Committee) 一種影片格式

2. PAL (=Phase Alternation Line) 一種影片格式

CD 2-06

★ all-region DVD player [`ɔl͵rɪdʒən `di `vi `di ͵pleɚ] *n.* 多區 DVD 光碟機

Friend: My friend got me a bunch of DVDs from Asia, but they're all region 3 DVDs.

You: Don't worry. You can watch them at the library. I think they have all-region DVD players.

朋友： 我朋友從亞洲帶了一堆 DVD 給我，但都是第三區的 DVD 光碟。

你： 別擔心。你可以到圖書館看，他們有多區 DVD 光碟機。

★ screen [skrin] *n.* 銀幕

You: Should we watch this documentary[1] in a TV room or the pro-jection room?

Friend: Let's get a projection room. The screen is a lot bigger.

你： 我們應該在電視室還是投影室看這卷紀錄片？

朋友： 我們去借間投影室。投影室的螢幕大得多。

★ remote control [rɪ`mot kən`trol] *n.* 遙控器

Friend: I can't see the buttons on this DVD player.

You: Where's the remote control? Use that instead.

朋友： 我看不見這台 DVD 光碟機的按鈕。

你： 遙控器在哪裡？改用那個好了。

[Word List]

1. documentary [͵dɑkjə`mɛntərɪ] *n.* 紀錄片

★ digital media lab [ˈdɪdʒɪtḷ ˈmidɪə ˌlæb] *n.* 數位媒體實習室

Friend: The library has a great digital media lab.

You: I know. You can take graphics design[1] lessons, and even learn how to edit digital video there.

朋友： 圖書館有一間很棒的數位媒體實習室。

你： 我知道。你可以在那兒上平面設計課，甚至還可以學剪輯數位影片。

★ table tent [ˈtebḷ ˌtɛnt] *n.* 桌上型紙板（帳篷狀）

You: Why is there a table tent on every table?

Friend: Student government elections are coming up.

你： 為什麼每張桌子上都有個帳篷狀紙板？

朋友： 因為學生政府的選舉快到了。

[Word List]

1. graphic design [ˈgræfɪk dɪˈzaɪn] *n.* 平面設計

The University Library

6th Floor

Library Administration¹ Offices	PT-PZ
Editing Projects	PQ1-499

5th Floor

Government Information Resources²		PR, PS
N, PM, PN	PH-PK	PL1-3602.T

4th Floor

Newspapers	Periodicals³	N, P-PG
Microforms⁴	J-JX5355.M	JX5355.N-JZ

3rd Floor

Special Collections	Special Exhibits	PQ500-999
E, F, G	D-DB955	DB956-DX

2nd Floor

Entrance	Reference⁵ Room	Q-Z
Circulation	Interlibrary Service	Coffee Shop

1st Floor

Copy Center	Book Arts	K, L
A, B, C	H-HC275	HC276-HX

Enterance is located on the 2nd floor.

[翻 譯]

大學圖書館

六樓

| 圖書館行政辦公室 | | PT-PZ |
| 編輯計畫 | | PQ 1-499 |

五樓

| 政府資訊資源 | | PR, PS |
| N, PM, PN | PH-PK | PL1-3602.T |

四樓

| 新聞 | 期刊 | N, P-PG |
| 微縮膠片 | J-JX5355.M | JX5355.N-JZ |

三樓

| 特殊館藏 | 特展 | PQ500-999 |
| E, F, G | D-DB955 | DB956-DX |

二樓

| 入口 | 參考書閱覽室 | Q-Z |
| 借還書櫃台 | 館際服務 | 咖啡廳 |

一樓

| 影印中心 | 圖書藝術 | K, L |
| A, B, C | H-HC275 | HC276-HX |

入口在二樓

[Word List]

1. administration [əd͵mɪnəˋstreʃən] *n.* 行政
2. resource [rɪˋsors] *n.* 資源
3. periodical [͵pɪrɪˋɑdɪk!] *n.* 期刊
4. microform [ˋmaɪkrə͵fɔrm] *n.* 微縮膠片
5. reference [ˋrɛfərəns] *n.* 參考書

留學 智慧王

Study Habits 唸書習慣

　　就如同每個人對音樂的喜好不同，唸書的習慣也會因人而異。有的人需要百分之百的安靜，因此唯一的選擇就是到圖書館的禁音樓層看書。有的人則偏好有一點聲音的地方，因此不介意是在有人講話的地方看書。有的人甚至需要把音樂放很大聲才能專心看書。最好能找出最適合自己的讀書方式。你可以先嘗試在幾種不同的地方唸書，然後找出效率最佳的環境。

How to Study Effectively 如何有效地學習

　　常有人建議大學生，每上一小時的課，課後就應該花兩小時唸書。很可笑嗎？不見得。大學生每學期平均要修大約 15 個學分（視學校而定），相當於 15 小時的課堂時間。這表示學生應該在課後花 30 小時看書。30 小時聽起來很多，但是美國大學要求學生在上課之前要看許多書。雖然大部分的學生並不見得會按照「每上一小時課，課後唸兩小時書」的原則，但你最好做好心理準備，得非常用功、看很多書，並有效地運用時間。

CD 2-07

Other Library Vocabulary 其他圖書館相關字彙

- library annex [`laɪˌbrɛrɪ `ænɛks]　　　　　*n.* 圖書館附屬樓
- interlibrary loan [ˌɪntɚ`laɪbrərɪ `lon]　　*n.* 館際借閱
- microfilm [`maɪkroˌfɪlm]　　　　　　　　*n.* 縮影膠片
- microfiche [`maɪkroˌfiʃ]　　　　　　　　*n.* 縮影單片
- non-circulating [nɑn`sɝkjəˌletɪŋ]　　　　*adj.* 不外借的
- off-site storage [`ɔfˌsaɪt `storɪʤ]　　　　*n.* 館外儲存
- card catalog [`kɑrd `kætḷˌɔg]　　　　　　*n.* 卡片目錄
- research librarian [`risɝtʃ laɪˌbrɛrɪən]　　*n.* 圖書館研究員
- current periodical [`kɝənt ˌpɪrɪ`ɑdɪkḷ]　　*n.* 最新期刊
- copy card [`kɑpɪ ˌkɑrd]　　　　　　　　*n.* 影印卡
- map room [`mæp ˌrum]　　　　　　　　*n.* 地圖室
- bar code [`bɑr ˌkod]　　　　　　　　　*n.* 條碼
- rare collection [`rɛr kə`lɛkʃən]　　　　　*n.* 罕見館藏
- return slip [rɪ`tɝn ˌslɪp]　　　　　　　　*n.* 還書條
- newspaper archive [`njuzˌpepɚ ˌɑrkaɪv]　*n.* 報紙檔案室
- bulletin board [`bʊlətṇ ˌbord]　　　　　*n.* 佈告欄

Chapter 8

Health 健康問題

What if I get sick?

A change in climate, living in close quarters, or just plain stress can cause anyone to get sick. For many international students, it's usually all of the above. Some students can avoid getting sick by eating healthy, getting enough exercise, and not staying up all night, but it can be difficult to properly take care of yourself while studying abroad. If you do get sick, most schools have a Student Health Center, where you can see a doctor.

生病了怎麼辦?

氣候變化、密閉的生活空間,甚或只是單純的壓力都可能讓人病倒。對許多外籍學生而言,以上所述通常全都是致病原因。有些學生可以靠吃得健康、充足的運動和不熬夜來避免生病,但是在國外唸書的時候,照顧好自己並非易事。如果你真的生病了,大部分的學校都有學生健康中心,可以去那裡看醫生。

Top 10 必會字彙

 CD **2-08**

★ **nausea**
['nɔzɪə]
n. 噁心

★ **vomit**
['vɑmɪt]
v. 嘔吐

★ **prescription**
[prɪ`skrɪpʃən]
n. 處方

★ **dosage**
['dosɪʤ]
n. 劑量

★ **drowsy**
['draʊzɪ]
adj. 睏的；想睡的

★ **swollen**
['swolən]
adj. 腫起來的

★ **sprain**
[spren]
n. 扭傷

★ **ankle brace**
['æŋkḷ ,bres]
n. 腳踝護具

★ **rash**
[ræʃ]
n. 疹子

★ **ointment**
['ɔɪntmənt]
n. 藥膏

CD 2-09

1 A: Can you describe your symptoms?

B: Mainly nausea and vomiting. I've also had a bad headache.

A: 你能不能描述一下你的症狀？

B: 主要是噁心和嘔吐。我的頭也很痛。

---

2 A: Will you give me a prescription?

B: Yes. Pay attention to the dosage. The medicine may make you drowsy.

A: 可不可以開藥給我？

B: 可以。請注意劑量，這藥會讓你昏昏欲睡。

---

3 A: Ouch! My ankle is really swollen.

B: It looks like a sprain. You're going to have to wear an ankle brace.

A: 哎喲！我的腳踝腫得好大。

B: 看來是扭傷了。你得戴腳踝護具。

---

4 A: I have a rash on my arm that won't go away.

B: Put some of this ointment on it. And don't scratch it!

A: 我手臂上起了個疹子，一直都退不掉。

B: 在上面塗一點這種藥膏。還有，不要抓！

你可以跟我這樣說

CD **2-10**

Dialogue A

Annie goes to the Student Health Center to get a meningitis shot.

Doctor: Annie Wang? You're here for a meningitis shot, right?

Annie:　That's right. Will it hurt? I really hate getting injections.

Doctor: It's just a small jab. Are you allergic to any medication?

Annie:　Yes, I'm allergic to penicillin.

Doctor: You shouldn't have any problems with the vaccine, but if there are any side effects, come right back to the health center.

Annie:　Do I need to get this vaccine every year?

Doctor: No, you only need one dose. I'm going to clean your skin with rubbing alcohol first. *(He injects the vaccine.)* All right, you're all set. Keep your arm bent for a couple of minutes to stop the bleeding.

Annie:　OK, thanks. By the way, doctor, I've been having a problem with my right ear. Things sound muffled.

Doctor: Let me take a look. Any pain?

Annie:　Yeah, my whole ear is a little sore.

Doctor: Looks like you've got a bit of an ear infection. I'll write a prescription for some eardrops and you can pick them up at the pharmacy before you leave. Have you been doing any swimming?

Annie:　Yes. I went to the pool over the weekend.

Doctor: Make sure you get the water out of your ears after you swim. You can put a couple of drops of alcohol in your ear if it feels like there's water trapped in it. Keep the alcohol in there for a few seconds, then tilt your head to drain it out.

Annie:　I'll try that. Thank you.

安妮到學生健康中心打腦膜炎疫苗。

醫生：安妮・王？妳是來打腦膜炎疫苗的，對嗎？

安妮：是的。會痛嗎？我最討厭打針了。

醫生：只是打個小針而已。妳有沒有對什麼藥物過敏？

安妮：有，我對盤尼西林過敏。

醫生：妳打這支疫苗應該不會有什麼問題，但是如果有任何副作用，馬上回來
　　　健康中心。

安妮：我每年都要打這疫苗嗎？

醫生：不需要，只要打一劑就好。我先用消毒用酒精幫妳清潔一下皮膚。*（他
　　　注射疫苗。）*好了，打好了。手臂保持彎曲幾分鐘，才不會流血。

安妮：好，謝謝。對了，醫生，我的右耳最近有點問題，聲音都聽不太清楚。

醫生：我看看。會痛嗎？

安妮：會，整隻耳朵都有點痛。

醫生：看來妳耳朵有點感染。我開一些耳藥水給妳，妳可以在離開前到藥局去
　　　拿。妳最近有去游泳嗎？

安妮：有，我週末去了游泳池。

醫生：游完泳後，務必將水清出耳朵。如果覺得耳朵裡面有水出不來的話，可
　　　以在耳朵裡滴兩三滴酒精，讓酒精在裡面停留幾秒，然後將頭傾斜，讓
　　　它流出來。

安妮：我會試試看的，謝謝你。

[Words & Phrases]

- meningitis [ˌmɛnɪnˈdʒaɪtɪs] *n.* 腦膜炎
- injection [ɪnˈdʒɛkʃən] *n.* 注射；打針
- jab [dʒæb] *n.* （口語）注射
- allergic [əˈlɝdʒɪk] *adj.* 過敏的
- penicillin [ˌpɛnɪˈsɪlɪn] *n.* 盤尼西林
- vaccine [ˈvæksin] *n.* 疫苗
- side effect [ˈsaɪd ɪ ˌfɛkt] *n.* 副作用
- rubbing alcohol [ˈrʌbɪŋ ˌælkəhɔl] *n.* 消
　毒用酒精
- muffled [ˈmʌfld] *adj.* （聲音）聽不太清
　楚的
- eardrops [ˈɪrˌdrɑps] *n.* 耳藥水
- pharmacy [ˈfɑrməsɪ] *n.* 藥局；藥房

你可以跟我這樣說

CD **2-11**

Dialogue B

Kevin has caught a cold and so his friend Peggy takes him to the drugstore.

Kevin: Achoo! I should go to the doctor.

Peggy: What for? It's just a cold. The drugstore has everything you need.

Kevin: Why don't Americans like going to the doctor?

Peggy: We go, but only when it's serious. A cold usually isn't serious enough to see a doctor. What are your symptoms?

Kevin: I have a sore throat and a fever.

Peggy: See, that sounds like an average cold. If you weren't able to get out of bed, then I'd take you to the doctor. You'll probably feel better in a day or two.

Kevin: But what about now? It hurts to swallow.

Peggy: That's why we're here at the drugstore. Look. These are throat lozenges. They'll help your sore throat. And you'll need some Tylenol Cold. Do you prefer tablets or capsules?

Kevin: What's Tylenol? *(He looks at the package.)* Oh, it's like Panadol. Um ... capsules, I guess. *(coughs)*

Peggy: Hmm ... sounds like you need some cough syrup as well. We'll pick up a bottle of that, and get you some vitamin C. And I'll make you some chicken soup later.

Kevin: Thanks Peggy. You're really sweet.

Peggy: Not a problem. We'll keep an eye on your symptoms. If you don't get better, or start feeling worse, I'll take you to the health center.

凱文感冒了，他的朋友珮姬帶他到藥局去。

凱文：哈啾！我應該去看醫生。

珮姬：為什麼？不過是個感冒罷了。你需要的藥藥局裡都有。

凱文：為什麼美國人不喜歡看醫生？

珮姬：我們看啊，但只有在症狀嚴重時才去。感冒通常不會嚴重到需要看醫
　　　生。你有哪些症狀？

凱文：我喉嚨痛，還發燒。

珮姬：看吧，聽起來像是普通感冒。如果你病到無法下床的話，我再帶你去看
　　　醫生。你大概一兩天之內就會覺得好多了。

凱文：可是現在呢？吞嚥時都會痛。

珮姬：我們來藥局就是為了這個呀。瞧，這些是喉錠，對你的喉嚨痛有幫助。
　　　你也需要泰樂諾感冒藥。你比較喜歡錠片還是膠囊？

凱文：泰樂諾是什麼？*（他看包裝。）*哦，就像普拿疼嘛。嗯⋯⋯我看還是膠
　　　囊吧。*（咳嗽）*

珮姬：嗯⋯⋯看來你還需要咳嗽糖漿。我們買一瓶糖漿，然後再幫你買些維他
　　　命 C。待會兒我做雞湯給你喝。

凱文：謝謝妳，珮姬，妳真好。

珮姬：小事一樁。我們要注意一下你的症狀。如果你沒有比較好，或是開始惡
　　　化的話，我再帶你去健康中心。

[Words & Phrases]

- drugstore [ˋdrʌɡˌstor] *n.* （常兼售化妝
  品等雜貨的）藥房
- symptom [ˋsɪmptəm] *n.* 徵狀
- sore [sor] *adj.* 疼痛發炎的
- fever [ˋfivɚ] *n.* 發燒
- swallow [ˋswɑlo] *v.* 吞嚥
- lozenge [ˋlɑzɪndʒ] *n.* （尤其指口含的）
  錠劑
- Tylenol [ˋtaɪlənɔl] *n.* 【商標】泰樂諾
  （止痛藥）
- tablet [ˋtæblɪt] *n.* 錠片
- capsule [ˋkæpsl] *n.* 膠囊
- Panadol [ˋpænədɔl] *n.* 【商標】普拿疼
  （止痛藥）
- cough syrup [ˋkɔf ˌsɪrəp] *n.* 咳嗽糖漿

超實用單字

 CD **2-12**

Symptoms and Health-Related Questions 症狀和與健康相關的問題

★ sleepy [ˋslipɪ] *adj.* **想睡的**

You: Does this medicine have any side effects?
Doctor: You might feel a little sleepy, so don't take it if you plan on driving.

你： 這個藥有沒有任何副作用？
醫生： 你可能會覺得有一點想睡，所以如果打算開車的話，就不要吃。

★ covered [ˋkʌvəd] *adj.* **有保險給付的**

You: Is this vaccine covered by insurance?[1]
Doctor: It is, but you have to pay $35 if you have private insurance.

你： 這種疫苗保險有沒有給付？
醫生： 有，但如果是私人保險，就必須付 35 美元。

★ stitch [stɪtʃ] *n.* **縫針**

You: I fell down the stairs and cut my head. Will I need stitches?
Nurse: You may need a few. We'll let the doctor take a look.

你： 我從樓梯上摔下來，撞破了頭。需要縫嗎？
護士： 可能需要縫幾針。我們讓醫生看一下吧。

[Word List]

1. insurance [ɪnˋʃurəns] *n.* 保險

☆ blood type [ˋblʌd ˏtaɪp] *n.* 血型

> Doctor: Do you know your blood type?
> You: Yes. I'm O positive.[1]

> 醫生： 你知道自己的血型嗎？
> 你：   知道，我是 O 型陽性。

At the Drugstore 藥局裡

★ geltab [ˋdʒɛlˏtæb] *n.* 囊錠

> You: What are geltabs?
> Friend: They look like tablets, but have a coating[2] like capsules.

> 你：   囊錠是什麼？
> 朋友： 它們看起來像錠片，但和膠囊一樣有一層外層。

★ thermometer [θəˋmɑmətɚ] *n.* 溫度計；體溫計

> You: Do I have a fever?
> Friend: I'm not sure. Let me get thermometer.

> 你：   我有沒有發燒？
> 朋友： 我不確定。我去拿體溫計。

[Word List]

1. positive [ˋpɑzətɪv] *adj.*【醫學】陽性的   2. coating [ˋkotɪŋ] *n.* 外層；披覆

CD **2-13**

⭐ over-the-counter medicine [`ovɚ ðə `kaʊntɚ `mɛdəsn̩] *n.* 成藥

You: Do you think I need to see the doctor?
Friend: No. Just get some over-the-counter medicine for your cold.

你：   你覺得我需不需要看醫生？
朋友：   不需要。你的感冒買一些成藥就好了。

⭐ eyedrops [`aɪ,drɑps] *n.* 眼藥水

You: I have really bad allergies[1] and my eyes itch[2] like crazy.
Pharmacist: You can try these eyedrops. They should relieve[3] the itching.

你：   我過敏非常嚴重，眼睛癢得要命。
藥劑師：   你可以試試這眼藥水，應該可以止癢。

⭐ Band-Aid [`bænd ,ed] *n.* OK 繃

You: I fell down and cut my leg. Do you have a Band-Aid?
Friend: Sure. Is one enough?

你：   我跌了一跤，腿刮破了。你有沒有 OK 繃？
朋友：   當然有。一個夠嗎？

[Word List]

1. allergy [`ælɚʤɪ] *n.* 過敏症

2. itch [ɪtʃ] *v.* 發癢

3. relieve [rɪ`liv] *v.* 減輕；緩和

⭐ indigestion [ˌɪndəˈdʒɛstʃən] *n.* 消化不良

You: My stomach really hurts.
Friend: It's probably just indigestion. You ate six slices[1] of pizza!

你： 我的肚子好痛。
朋友： 八成只是消化不良。你吃了六片披薩耶！

⭐ antacid tablet [æntˈæsɪd ˈtæblɪt] *n.* 制酸錠

Friend: Ugh ... I feel sick. I think I ate too much.
You: Here, take some antacid tablets.

朋友： 呃……我不舒服。我想是吃太多了。
你： 來，吃幾片制酸錠吧。

[**Word List**]

1. slice [slaɪs] *n.* 切片；薄片

留學　佈告欄

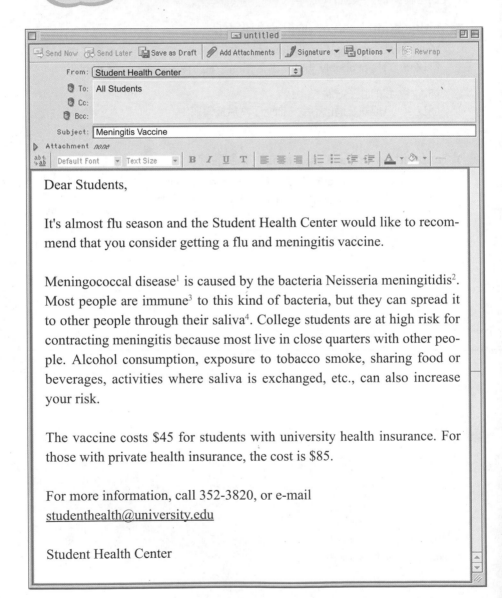

---
untitled

Send Now　Send Later　Save as Draft　Add Attachments　Signature ▼　Options ▼　Rewrap

From: Student Health Center

To: All Students

Cc:

Bcc:

Subject: Meningitis Vaccine

▷ Attachment *none*

Default Font ▼　Text Size ▼　**B** *I* U T ｜ ≡ ≡ ≡ ｜ ≣ ≣ 崖 崖 ｜ A ▼ ◇ ▼ ｜ —

Dear Students,

It's almost flu season and the Student Health Center would like to recommend that you consider getting a flu and meningitis vaccine.

Meningococcal disease[1] is caused by the bacteria Neisseria meningitidis[2]. Most people are immune[3] to this kind of bacteria, but they can spread it to other people through their saliva[4]. College students are at high risk for contracting meningitis because most live in close quarters with other people. Alcohol consumption, exposure to tobacco smoke, sharing food or beverages, activities where saliva is exchanged, etc., can also increase your risk.

The vaccine costs $45 for students with university health insurance. For those with private health insurance, the cost is $85.

For more information, call 352-3820, or e-mail studenthealth@university.edu

Student Health Center

[翻 譯]

寄件人：學生健康中心
收件人：所有學生
主旨：　腦膜炎疫苗

各位同學：

流感季即將開始，學生健康中心建議您考慮施打流感和腦膜炎混和疫苗。

腦膜炎由腦膜炎雙球菌所引起。多數人對這種細菌有免疫力，但卻可能經由唾液傳染給他人。大學生多與人處於密閉的生活空間中，因此是感染腦膜炎的高危險群。飲酒、吸二手菸、共食或共飲及其他互通唾液之行為等，都會增加危險性。

持有校園健保的學生，疫苗費用為 45 美元；私人健保的學生則為 85 美元。

如需其他資訊，請來電 352-3820 或將電子郵件寄至
studenthealth@university.edu

學生健康中心

[Word List]

1. meningococcal disease [ˌmɛnɪŋgə`kɑkḷ dɪ`ziz] n. 腦膜炎（疾病名）
2. bacteria Neisseria meningitidis [bæk`tɪrɪə naɪ`sɪrɪə mɛnɪʤaɪ`taɪdɪs] n. 腦膜炎雙球菌（奈瑟氏菌）
3. immune [ɪ`mjun] adj. 免疫的
4. saliva [sə`laɪvə] n. 唾液

留學 智慧王

Health Insurance 健康保險

　　大部分的大學會規定所有的學生都必須投保健康險。通常你可以選擇透過大學或向私人保險公司購買健康險。如果你投保學校的健康險，到學生健康中心看病會比較方便，打疫苗和拿藥時也會比較便宜。

Should I Go See a Doctor? 我該去看醫生嗎？

　　和台灣人不同的是，美國人不會每次生病都去看醫生。如果受涼了或感染流行性感冒，他們會到藥局購買成藥，等病自然痊癒。除非絕對必要，否則美國醫生不會開藥給你。因為看病很貴，保險費很高，這也使得美國人比較少看醫生。

CD 2-14

Symptoms and Over-the-Counter Remedies 症狀與成藥

symptom 症狀	medicine 藥名	type/description 類型／描述
cold [kold] n. 感冒	Vicks Dayquil [ˋvɪks ˋdekwɪl] n. 維克戴奎爾綜合感冒藥（日用） Vicks Nyquil [ˋvɪks ˋnaɪkwɪl] n. 維克奈奎爾綜合感冒藥（夜用）	cold medicine [ˋkold ˏmɛdəsn̩] n. 感冒藥
cough [kɔf] n. 咳嗽	Cepacol [ˋsɛpəkɔl] n. 瑟培可糖錠	cough remedy [ˋkɔf ˏrɛmədɪ] n. 咳嗽藥
headache [ˋhɛdˏek] n. 頭痛	Aleve [ˋæliv] n. 艾力弗藥丸 Excedrin [ɪkˋsɛdrɪn] n. 伊克賽錠	pain medicine [ˋpen ˏmɛdəsn̩] n. 止痛藥

menstrual discomfort [ˈmɛnstruəl dɪsˈkʌmfət] n. 經期症狀	Midol [ˈmaɪdl] n. 美多錠	pain reliever [ˈpen rɪˌlivə] n. 止痛劑
muscle ache [ˈmʌsl ˌek] n. 肌肉痠痛	Bengay [bɛnˈge] n. 奔肌乳膏	topical ointment [ˈtɑpɪkl ˈɔɪntmənt] n. 局部外用藥膏
stomach ache [ˈstʌmək ˌek] n. 胃痛	Pepto-Bismol [ˈpɛptəˈbɪzmɔl] n. 百託必司模胃藥	stomach remedy [ˈstʌmək ˌrɛmɛdɪ] n. 胃藥
indigestion [ˌɪndəˈdʒɛstʃən] n. 消化不良	Alka Seltzer [ˈælkəˈsɛltsə] n. 我可舒適錠	dyspepsia remedy [dɪˈspɛpʃə ˌrɛmədɪ] n. 消化劑
heartburn [ˈhɑrtˌbɝn] n. 胃灼熱	Rolaids [ˈroledz] n. 若雷氏制酸劑	antacid [æntˈæsɪd] n. 抗酸劑
constipation [ˌkɑnstəˈpeʃən] n. 便秘	Correctol [kəˈrɛktɔl] n. 可瑞妥瀉劑	laxative [ˈlæksətɪv] n. 瀉藥
diarrhea [ˌdaɪəˈriə] n. 腹瀉	Imodium AD [ɪˈmodɪəm ˈeˈdi] n. 痢達膠囊	antidiarrheal medication [ˌæntaɪˌdaɪəˈriəl ˌmɛdɪˈkeʃən] n. 止瀉藥
insect bite [ˈɪnsɛkt ˌbaɪt] n. 蚊蟲咬傷	After Bite [ˈæftə ˌbaɪt] n. 蚊蟲叮咬擦劑	insect bite ointment [ˈɪnsɛkt ˌbaɪt ˌɔɪntmənt] n. 蚊蟲咬傷藥膏
itchiness [ˈɪtʃɪnɪs] n. 癢	Cortaid [ˈkɔtˌed] n. 克泰止癢軟膏	anti-itch cream [ˈæntaɪˈɪtʃ ˈkrim] n. 止癢膏
sunburn [ˈsʌnˌbɝn] n. 曬傷	Solarcaine [ˈsoləˌken] n. 速樂康噴霧	burn spray [ˈbɝn ˌspre] n. 曬／燙傷噴劑
hay fever [ˈhe ˌfivə] n. 花粉熱 allergy [ˈælədʒɪ] n. 過敏	Benadryl [ˈbɛnədrɪl] n. 派德抗組織胺藥	anti-histamine [ˈæntaɪˈhɪstəˌmin] n. 抗組胺劑

Chapter 9

Exploring Your Area and Taking Trips

熟悉環境和旅遊

Exploring the area around your school

Studying overseas can be an exciting experience, particularly if you take the opportunity to explore the area around your school, in addition to traveling around the country you are staying in. It doesn't matter if your university is located in a big city, in a college town, or in the countryside, taking part in local activities and events will just make your years abroad even more memorable!

熟悉學校環境

出國留學可以是令人興奮的經驗；除了環遊你所待的國家外，如果你能把握機會探索學校附近的區域，那就更棒了。無論你的學校是在大都市、大學城或在鄉間都無所謂，參與當地的活動和盛會將會使你在國外的生活更值得回憶！

Top 10 必會字彙

 CD **2-15**

⭐1 **winery**
[ˋwaɪnərɪ]

n. 酒莊；釀酒廠

⭐2 **wine tasting**
[ˋwaɪn ˏtestɪŋ]

n. 品酒

⭐3 **picnic**
[ˋpɪknɪk]

n. 野餐

⭐4 **rock climbing**
[ˋrɑk ˏklaɪmɪŋ]

n. 攀岩

⭐5 **hiking**
[ˋhaɪkɪŋ]

n. 健行

⭐6 **inner tubing**
[ˋɪnɚ ˏtjubɪŋ]

n. 坐內胎漂浮

⭐7 **highway**
[ˋhaɪˏwe]

n. 公路

⭐8 **speed trap**
[ˋspid ˏtræp]

n. 測速照相

⭐9 **motel**
[moˋtɛl]

n. 汽車旅館

⭐10 **bed and breakfast**
[ˋbɛd ənd ˋbrɛkfəst]

n. 供住宿與早餐的飯店（常B&B）

1 A: Let's go to the winery and do some wine tasting this weekend.

B: Sure. And we can have a picnic near the winery.

A: 咱們這個週末到酒莊去品酒吧。

B: 好啊。我們還可以在酒莊附近野餐。

---

2 A: Jim wants to go to Cowles Creek and do some rock climbing.

B: I've been there. It's also great for hiking and inner tubing.

A: 吉姆想去克渥斯溪攀岩。

B: 我去過克渥斯溪,那裡也很適合健行和坐內胎漂浮。

---

3 A: Slow down! We just passed a cop!

B: I hate this highway. There are so many speed traps.

A: 開慢點!我們剛跟條子擦身而過!

B: 我討厭這條公路,有好多測速照相。

---

4 A: Are you and your boyfriend going to stay in a motel?

B: We've got more class than that! We're staying in a bed and breakfast.

A: 你和男朋友會住汽車旅館嗎?

B: 我們的層級比那個高!我們會住供住宿和早餐的飯店。

你可以跟我這樣說

 CD 2-17

Dialogue A

Annie and Liz go apple picking.

Annie: Why are we going apple picking? Isn't it just easier to buy apples from the supermarket?

Liz: Apple picking is fun! You get to choose your own apples. And they have so many varieties. Besides, they sell apple cider and doughnuts at the orchard.

Annie: What's apple cider?

Liz: It's a drink made from apples that's usually served hot with a bit of cinnamon.

Annie: Hmm ...sounds interesting. So, will we have to climb up the trees?

Liz: *(laughs)* No! They give you these poles with a basket attached. You use it to twist the apple off the tree and it falls right into your basket! I'm going to buy some apples to make apple pie and apple crumble!

Annie: The flyer says they have hayrides at the orchard. What's a hayride?

Liz: You ride in a horse-drawn wagon filled with hay.

Annie: And that's supposed to be fun?

Liz: It's just part of the fun. Remember, the real purpose of this trip is to get away from the campus and learn something new. It's important to get out there and mix with the locals.

Annie: When in Rome, do as the Romans do?

Liz: Exactly. Now trust me, you'll enjoy the hayride. And if you don't, I'll buy you another doughnut!

安妮和莉姿去採蘋果。

安妮：我們幹嘛去採蘋果？到超市買蘋果不是更方便嗎？

莉姿：採蘋果很好玩呀！妳可以自己挑蘋果。他們的蘋果種類很多，而且他們還會在果園賣蘋果西打和甜甜圈。

安妮：蘋果西打是什麼？

莉姿：是一種蘋果做的飲料，通常裡面會放一點肉桂，當熱飲喝。

安妮：嗯⋯⋯聽起來滿有意思的。那我們需要爬到蘋果樹上嗎？

莉姿：（笑）不用！他們會給妳綁著籃子的竿子，妳用竿子把蘋果從果樹上扭下來，蘋果就會剛好掉進籃子裡！我要買一些蘋果做蘋果派和蘋果奶酥！

安妮：廣告傳單上說果園有稻草車。什麼叫稻草車？

莉姿：就是乘坐載滿稻草的無篷馬車。

安妮：那很好玩嗎？

莉姿：那只是好玩的一部分而已。記住，此行的真正目是走出校園，學習一些新的東西。重要的是到校外，融入當地人的生活。

安妮：就是說入境隨俗囉？

莉姿：正是。相信我，妳會喜歡坐稻草車的。要是妳覺得不好玩，我就再請妳吃一個甜甜圈！

[Words & Phrases]

- apple cider [`æpḷ ˏsaɪdɚ] *n.* 蘋果西打
- doughnut [`donət] *n.* 甜甜圈
- orchard [`ɔrtʃɚd] *n.* 果園
- cinnamon [`sɪnəmən] *n.* 肉桂
- pole [pol] *n.* 棍；竿
- attached [ə`tætʃt] *adj.* 繫住的；綁住的
- twist [twɪst] *v.* 扭動；轉動
- apple crumble [`æpḷ ˏkrʌmbḷ] *n.* 蘋果奶酥
- flyer [`flaɪɚ] *n.* 廣告傳單
- hayride [`heˏraɪd] *n.* 坐稻草車
- horse-drawn [`hɔrs ˏdrɔn] *adj.* 用馬拉的
- wagon [`wægən] *n.* 無篷馬車
- be supposed to 應該；一般認為
- mix with （與別人融洽）相處
- local [`lokḷ] *n.* 當地居民；本地人（常用複數）
- When in Rome, do as Romans do. 入境隨俗。

你可以跟我這樣說

 CD 2-18

Dialogue B

Kevin is taking a road trip to Atlantic City with his friends.

Brian: OK. This bag is ready to put in the car. It's got snacks, water, and my MP3 player to provide the soundtrack for this road trip.

Kevin: This is great! I've never been to Atlantic City before. How long is the drive going to be?

Brian: About seven hours. We'll take a break about halfway there. I can't wait to hit the slots.

Kevin: You lose too much money on slot machines. I may not play.

Brian: You can't go to Atlantic City and not gamble! It's all part of the adventure of the road trip. Come on, I thought Taiwanese were big gamblers!

Kevin: Well, maybe I'll play a little blackjack and roulette.

Brian: Now you're talking! Do you know how to play craps?

Kevin: Nah. It seems kind of complicated. What else is there to do in Atlantic City?

Brian: All the major casinos are on the boardwalk. The hotels aren't as cool as those in Las Vegas. Some people find it gaudy, but it's just fun. Just taking a stroll and checking out the people can be pretty fun.

Kevin: Peggy asked me to buy her some saltwater taffy. She said that it's candy. Is it actually salty?

Brian: Dude, you've never had saltwater taffy before? No, it's not salty! Oh, we better hit the road if we want to get there before dinner.

Kevin: All right, let's go! I call shotgun!

凱文要和朋友一起做公路旅遊，到大西洋城去。

布萊恩：好。這袋可以放上車了，裡面有點心、水和我的 MP3 隨身聽，可以為這趟公路之旅提供音樂。

凱文：　真棒！我從來沒去過大西洋城。開車大概要多久？

布萊恩：大約七小時。我們中途會休息一下，我等不及要玩吃角子老虎了。

凱文：　玩吃角子老虎會輸很多錢，我可能不會玩。

布萊恩：哪有人去大西洋城不賭博的！這就是公路之旅刺激的地方。少來了，我還以為台灣人都很愛賭博呢！

凱文：　嗯，或許我會玩一下二十一點和輪盤賭吧。

布萊恩：這才是嘛！你知不知道怎麼玩雙骰子？

凱文：　不知。似乎有點複雜。大西洋城還有什麼好玩的？

布萊恩：所有主要的賭場都在木板道上。那裡的旅館沒有拉斯維加斯的酷。有些人覺得大西洋城華麗而俗氣，但就是玩嘛。光是溜達溜達，看看人群也會很好玩。

凱文：　珮姬叫我幫她買鹽水太妃糖，她說那是一種糖果。真的是鹹的嗎？

布萊恩：老兄，你從來沒有吃過鹹水太妃糖？不，不是鹹的！噢，如果想在晚餐前到達的話，最好趕緊上路了。

凱文：　好，走吧！我要坐前座。

[Words & Phrases]

- soundtrack [`saʊnd͵træk] *n.* 音軌
- hit the slots　玩吃角子老虎
- slot machine [`slɑt mə͵ʃin] *n.* 吃角子老虎機
- blackjack [`blæk͵ʤæk] *n.* 二十一點
- roulette [ru`lɛt] *n.* 輪盤賭
- craps [kræps] *n.* 雙骰子賭博遊戲
- complicated [`kɑmplə͵ketɪd] *adj.* 複雜的
- casino [kə`sino] *n.* 賭場
- boardwalk [`bord͵wɔk] *n.* 木板道
- gaudy [`gɔdɪ] *adj.* 華麗而俗氣的
- saltwater taffy [`sɔlt͵wɔtɚ `tæfɪ] *n.* 鹹水太妃糖
- dude [djud] *n.* 傢伙；老兄
- hit the road　上路
- call shotgun [`ʃɑt͵gʌn] 指坐駕駛座旁邊的位子（古時坐馬車時，做此位子的人通常會拿一把獵槍，以保護馬車內的人）

留學　超實用字彙

CD 2-19

Weekend Activities 週末活動

★ kayak [`kaɪæk] v. 划小艇（kayak 原指愛斯基摩人的皮艇）

Friend: Have you ever been kayaking?
You:　No, but I've canoed.[1]

朋友：　你有沒有划過小艇？
你：　　沒有，但我划過獨木舟。

★ snowboard [`snoˌbord] v. 玩滑雪板

You:　　I can't wait to go snowboarding.
Friend: This ski trip is going to be a lot of fun.

你：　　我等不及要玩滑雪板了。
朋友：　這趟滑雪之旅一定會很好玩。

★ historical sites [hɪs`tɔrɪkḷ ˌsaɪts] n. 古蹟

Friend: Do you want to check out Monticello[2], Thomas Jefferson's home?
You:　　Sure, I love visiting historical sites.

朋友：　你要不要到蒙提薩羅，看一看湯瑪士‧傑弗遜的家？
你：　　好啊，我最喜歡看古蹟了。

[Word List]

1. canoe [kə`nu] v. 划獨木舟

2. Monticello [`mɑntɪˌtʃɛlo] n. 蒙提薩羅
   （位於美國維吉尼亞州）

★④ fair [fɛr] *n.* 市集

You: Is the fair going to be any fun?

Friend: Of course! There will be a ton of games to play and we can eat cotton candy[1], hot dogs, and taffy apples[2] ...

你：   市集好玩嗎？

朋友：當然！那裡有超多遊戲可以玩的，我們還可以吃棉花糖、熱狗、太妃糖蘋果⋯⋯

★⑤ car camping [ˈkɑr ˌkæmpɪŋ] *n.* 汽車露營

You: I heard that you're planning on going car camping this weekend? Are you going to sleep in the car?

Friend: No. We go to a campground[3] where you can park the car in the campsite[4] and you sleep in a tent.[5] You should come with us.

你：   我聽說你們這個週末打算去汽車露營？你們要睡車上嗎？

朋友：沒。我們去營地，車子可以停在那，你們就可以睡帳篷裡。你們應該跟我們去的。

★⑥ hibernate [ˈhaɪbɚˌnet] *v.* 蟄居；避寒

Friend: Hey, do you have any plans for this weekend? Want to come hiking?

You: No, thanks. I'm exhausted. I just plan to hibernate this weekend. Wake me up on Monday!

朋友：嘿，這個週末有沒有什麼計畫？要去健行嗎？

你：   不，謝了。我累斃了。我這週末打算閉關。禮拜一再把我叫醒吧！

[Word List]

1. cotton candy [ˈkɑtn̩ ˈkændɪ] *n.* 棉花糖
2. taffy apple [ˈtæfɪ ˌæpl̩] *n.* 外面包有一層太妃糖的蘋果
3. campground [ˈkæmpˌgraʊd] *n.* 營地
4. campsite [ˈkæmpˌsaɪt] *n.* 營地
5. tent [tɛnt] *n.* 帳篷

CD 2-20

Road Trips and Destinations 公路旅遊與目的地

⭐ drive-thru [ˋdraɪvˌθru] *n.* 得來速

Friend: Are you hungry?
You: Yup. There's a drive-thru up ahead.

朋友： 你餓不餓？
你： 餓。前方有得來速。

⭐ flat tire [ˌflæt ˋtaɪr] *n.* 輪胎沒氣；爆胎

Friend: Uh-oh! I think we have a flat tire.
You: Do we have a spare in the trunk?

朋友： 糟糕！我想有個輪胎好像沒氣了。
你： 我們車廂裡有沒有備胎？

⭐ car game [ˋkɑrˌgem] *n.* 汽車遊戲（指在車上玩的遊戲）

You: What are we going to do in the car for seven hours?
Friend: Don't worry. We'll listen to music, talk, and play a few car games.

你： 我們七個小時在車子裡要幹嘛？
朋友： 別擔心，我們可以聽音樂、聊天、玩幾個汽車遊戲。

★ rest stop [`rɛst ˌstap] *n.* **休息站**

You: Ah, man! You missed the rest stop. I've really got to use the restroom!

Friend: I'm sorry. I'll pull over¹ at the next gas station.

你： 啊，老天！你錯過了休息站。我真的很想上廁所！

朋友： 對不起。到了下個加油站的時候，我會靠邊停。

★ aquarium [ə`kwɛrɪəm] *n.* **水族館**

You: What can we do in San Diego?²

Friend: We can go to the zoo and the Birch Aquarium.³

你： 聖地牙哥有什麼好玩的？

朋友： 我們可以去動物園和波奇水族館。

[Word List]

1. pull over 靠邊停

2. San Diego [ˌsændi`ego] *n.* 聖地牙哥
（位於美國加州）

3. Birch Aquarium [`bɝtʃ ə`kwɛrɪəm] *n.*
波奇水族館（位於聖地牙哥市區北方）

留學 佈告欄

Carver's Mountain

APPLE PICKING!
HAYRIDES!

Mon.-Fri. 10 a.m.-5 p.m.
Sat.-Sun. 10 a.m.-7 p.m.

Take 8th Street to Interstate[1] 20. Turn left at Carver's Mountain.

[翻　譯]

卡弗之山

採蘋果！

搭乘稻草車！

週一到週五　早上 10 點至傍晚 5 點
週六至週日　早上 10 點至晚上 7 點

從第八街直行至 20 號州際公路，到了卡弗之山後左轉。

[Word List]

1. interstate [ˌɪntɚˋstet] *n.* 州際公路

留學 智慧王

Day Trip Ideas 當日來回的旅遊點子

由於學生平日忙於課業，可能會忘了學校之外還有很多好玩的事情可以做。位於小城市或大學城的學校尤其如此，因為這些地方比較孤立，和外界較少接觸。花一點時間探索並參加當地的活動，有助於體驗道地的留學生活。到當地的古蹟、旅遊勝地或酒莊走一遭吧，不要每個週末只到最近的購物中心或電影院消磨時間。到外面去好好地玩吧！

Road Trip "Musts" and Tips 公路旅遊注意事項和建議

學生很喜歡公路旅遊，因為可以開車到目的地，而不是花錢買飛機票。公路旅遊特別好玩，因為長時間坐在車內，是和好朋友相處的最佳時機。

幾個公路旅遊時該注意的事項與建議：

★ 確定帶了 CD、MP3 等以便聽音樂。

★ 永遠讓最有經驗的人開車。

★ 開長途的話，輪流開車。

★ 規劃好路線──可以利用提供路線圖的網站，如 www.mapquest.com。

★ 帶點心和水。

★ 如果開很多部車，趁休息時換車坐。如此一來，你可以和每個人都有相處的時間。

★ 為旅程多留一些時間──不要趕路！

★ 每部車中需有一支手機。

Car Games 汽車遊戲

★ 20 個問題（Twenty Questions）

指定一個人當鬼，請他默想車內的某樣東西。玩家輪流提問題，猜那是什

麼東西，但「鬼」只能回答是或不是。如果有玩家已經問了 20 個問題都還沒猜到，就該那名玩家當「鬼」。不然原來的「鬼」就得重新想一個東西。

★ 分類遊戲（Categories）

第一個玩家選出一種東西，比方說「花」。然後按照順時針方向，車內每個玩家輪流說出一個不同的花名。例如，第一個玩家說「玫瑰花」，下一個說「鬱金香」，然後下一個說「黃水仙」。如果玩家想不出不同種的花名，或是講出來的花名有重複，就算出局。贏家（最後一個說得出不同花名的參與者）可選擇下一個類別。

建議類別：農場動物、汽車、州名、顏色、水果、電視節目、電影、流行歌曲等。

★ 神秘嘉賓（Mystery Guest）

這個遊戲有兩種玩法，一個比較容易，可以和小孩玩，另一個較富挑戰性，可以給較大的小孩和大人玩。

簡單版中，當「鬼」的玩家假裝自己是「神秘佳賓」，例如聖誕老公公或祖父或是隔壁家的小貓。其他參與者輪流提問，想辦法猜出神秘嘉賓是誰。如：「你和我們住同一條街上嗎？」或「你有沒有雪花般的長鬍子？」等問題可幫助年幼的小朋友較容易掌握住正確方向。

猜出神秘嘉賓是誰的人可當「鬼」，重新主持下一輪的遊戲。如果是大一點的小孩和成人玩這個遊戲，神秘嘉賓可以是某個名人，不論是活的、死的或小說中的人物都可以。

chapter 10

Chapter 10

Clubs, Societies, and the Greek System

社團、協會與希臘系統

Get involved!

Sure, you're going overseas to study, but part of your "education" should include extracurricular activities that allow you to make friends, deal with new situations, and grow as a person. Most schools have a wide variety of clubs and organizations, so there's something for everyone. Students in various parts of the world are used to being involved in school activities, and some take part in university organizations to develop their leadership skills. To have the true "college experience abroad," get involved!

讓自己置身其中！

沒錯，你出國是為了唸書，但「留學教育」還應該包括課外活動，讓你結交朋友、處理從未碰到過的狀況並成為一個有用的人。大部分學校的社團和組織種類繁多，因此每個人一定都找得到適合自己的去參加。世界各地的學生習慣參與學校活動，更有人為了培養自己的領導能力而加入大學組織。為體驗真正的「國外大學經驗」，讓自己置身於各種活動中吧！

TOP 10 必會字彙

CD **2-21**

★ **activities fair**
[æk`tɪvətɪz ˌfɛr]
n. 活動展覽會

★ **intramural sports (IM sports)**
[ˌɪntrə`mjurəl `sports]
n. 校內運動競賽

★ **student government**
[`stjudṇt `gʌvəmənt]
n. 學生政府

★ **fundraiser**
[`fʌndˌrezəˑ]
n. 募款會

★ **ice-cream social**
[`aɪs ˌkrim `soʃəl]
n. 冰淇淋聯誼會（常為募款而舉辦）

★ **haze**
[hez]
v. 欺侮；戲弄（新生）

★ **ritual**
[`rɪtʃuəl]
n. 儀式

★ **rush**
[rʌʃ]
v. 爭取加入；招受新生

★ **service fraternity**
[`sɝvɪs frəˌtɝnətɪ]
n. 服務兄弟會

★ **business fraternity**
[`bɪznɪs frəˌtɝnətɪ]
n. 商業兄弟會

1
A: Are you going to the activities fair on Friday?

B: Yeah. I want to find out more about intramural sports on campus.

A: 你星期五要去活動展覽會嗎？

B: 是啊。我想多了解一下學校的校內運動競賽。

2
A: The student government is having a fundraiser next week. Want to go?

B: If it's an ice-cream social, then count me in.

A: 學生政府下星期有個募款會。要去嗎？

B: 如果是冰淇淋聯誼會的話，那就算我一份。

3
A: Another fraternity got caught hazing its pledges. It should be illegal.

B: I disagree. It's an important ritual and tradition of the Greek system.

A: 又有一個兄弟會被抓到欺負立誓加入的會員。這應該屬非法行為。

B: 我不同意。這是希臘系統中重要的儀式和傳統。

4
A: I'm going to rush that service fraternity.

B: Really? I thought you were going to join the business fraternity.

A: 我要爭取加入服務兄弟會。

B: 真的嗎？我以為你要加入商業兄弟會。

你可以跟我這樣說

CD **2-23**

Dialogue A

Kevin decides to join the Chinese Scholars Association.

Xiaolu: Hi, my name's Xiaolu. I'm the president of CSA. Welcome to our general meeting!

Kevin: Thanks. I'm Kevin. So, what are we going to do today?

Xiaolu: Well, we'll be collecting this semester's dues and talking about our upcoming events. Are you already a paid member of CSA?

Kevin: No, I'm not. That's why I'm here. I want to learn some more about CSA. What's the membership fee for?

Xiaolu: Well, if you pay dues, some of our events are free, or you get a discount.

Kevin: And what kinds of activities do you all plan?

Xiaolu: We have our biggest event coming up next month. It's our Chinese New Year celebration. We put on a show, have Chinese food, and there's always an after-party. We also put on a mah-jongg event, and we try to have a film night at least once a semester. And, even though we're "scholars," we have a carwash every spring.

Kevin: Sounds cool. How many members are there?

Xiaolu: We have about sixty paid members, and there are ten officers. We're one of the largest cultural organizations on campus. It's a lot of fun, so I hope you get involved!

Kevin: Thanks! I'm looking forward to meeting everyone.

Xiaolu: Well, take a seat. The meeting is about to get underway.

凱文決定參加中國學者協會。

小呂：嗨，我叫小呂，是中國學者協會的會長。歡迎參加我們的會員大會！

凱文：謝謝，我是凱文。那，我們今天打算做些什麼？

小呂：嗯，我們要收這學期的會費並談談即將舉辦的活動。你已經是中國學者協會的付費會員了嗎？

凱文：不，我不是。這正是我為什麼來這的原因。我想多知道一些中國學者協會的事。為什麼要繳會費？

小呂：嗯，如果你有繳會費，部分活動可免費參加，或者享有折扣。

凱文：那你們都籌備哪些活動？

小呂：我們最大的活動下個月即將登場，是我們的中國新年慶祝活動。我們會有表演、享用中國食物，而且會後一定會舉辦派對。我們也會有麻將活動，而且我們盡量至少每學期舉辦一次電影之夜。還有，雖然我們是「學者」，我們每年春季都會舉辦洗車活動。

凱文：聽起來很酷。你們有多少會員？

小呂：我們大約有 60 名付費會員和 10 名幹部。我們是校內最大的文化組織之一。很好玩，所以希望你加入！

凱文：謝謝！我很期待和大家見面。

小呂：嗯，坐一下。大會就快開始了。

[Words & Phrases]

- Chinese Scholars Association
  [tʃaɪˋniz skɑlɚz əˌsosɪˋeʃən] *n.* 中國學者協會
- general meeting [ˋdʒɛnərəl ˋmitɪŋ] *n.* 會員大會
- membership fee [ˋmɛmbɚˌʃɪp ˌfi] *n.* 會費
- put on 上演；辦（節目）

- after-party ……之後的派對
- mah-jongg [ˋmɑ ˋdʒɔŋ] *n.* 麻將
- carwash [ˋkɑrˌwɑʃ] *n.* 洗車（活動）
- officer [ˋɔfɪsɚ] *n.* 幹部
- cultural organization [ˋkʌltʃərəl ˌɔrgənəˋzeʃən] *n.* 文化組織
- underway [ˋʌndɚˌwe] *adj.* 在進行中的

你可以跟我這樣說

CD **2-24**

Dialogue B

Annie and Liz decide to take part in Rush Week.

Mary: Hi girls. My name is Mary Sanderford and I'm this year's Rush Coordinator. Rush is the selection process to enter a sorority and it lasts an entire week. Does anyone have any questions?

Annie: I don't really know about the Greek System. Why is it a good idea to rush?

Mary: Well, being part of a sorority is an amazing experience. You make lifelong friends, take part in fun social events, and are a part of history and tradition.

Liz: So how does Rush Week work?

Mary: You'll all be split into groups, and each group is assigned a Rush leader, called a Rho Chi. Then, you're taken to every sorority house. You'll meet all the sisters, and then they'll decide which rushees they will invite back. If you're invited back to a sorority, you'll attend their theme party. Afterwards, you get to choose up to three sororities you would like to pledge. If one of those three sororities would like to accept you, you're in!

Annie: What happens if you become a pledge?

Mary: You'll become a probationary member, and then go through initiation, which is the process of becoming a full-fledged member. Okay, girls. Please fill out these forms and I'll start assigning you to a Rho Chi. Good luck!

安妮和莉姿決定參加新生招收週的活動。

瑪莉：嗨，姊妹們。我叫瑪莉・山德福特，是本年度新生招收會的共同總招
　　　集。新生招收會是一個進入姐妹會的挑選過程，這個活動會持續一整
　　　週。有沒有人有問題？

安妮：我對希臘系統所知並不多。加入有什麼好處？

瑪莉：嗯，能成為姊妹會的一員是個不可多得的經驗。妳會結交到一輩子的朋
　　　友、參加好玩的社交活動，並成為歷史和傳統的一部分。

莉姿：新生招收週是怎麼樣運作的呢？

瑪莉：妳們會被分成幾個小組，每組分配一名新生招收隊長，叫做「新生招收
　　　輔導員」。然後妳們會被帶去各個姊妹會的會館，認識所有的姊妹，之
　　　後她們會決定邀請哪些新生候選人回來。如果妳被邀請回某個姊妹會，
　　　妳就可以參加他們的主題派對。之後至多可以選擇三個想立誓加入的姊
　　　妹會。如果這三個姊妹會中有一個想收妳，妳就進啦！

安妮：成為立誓加入的會員之後會怎樣？

瑪莉：妳會成為實習會員，然後妳必須完成全部的入會儀式，也就是成為正式
　　　會員的過程。好了，各位，請把這些表格填好，我會開始幫妳們分配新
　　　生招收輔導員。祝好運！

[Words & Phrases]

- Rush [rʌʃ] *n.* 新生招收
- coordinator [koˋɔrdn̩ˌetɚ] *n.* 協調者
- sorority [səˋrɔrətɪ] *n.* 姊妹會；女學生聯誼會
- Rho Chi [ˋro ˌkaɪ] *n.* 新生招收輔導員（每個新生招收輔導員都是姊妹會的會員，新生招收週期間，她們必須保持中立，以免新生對輔導員的姊妹會有先入為主的印象）
- rushee [rʌˋʃi] *n.* 新生會員候選人
- theme party [ˋθim ˋpɑrtɪ] *n.* 主題派對
- up to 至多……
- pledge [plɛdʒ] *v.* 立誓；宣誓
- probationary [proˋbeʃənˌɛrɪ] *adj.* 試用的；實習中的
- initiation [ɪˌnɪʃɪˋeʃən] *n.* 入會儀式
- full-fledged [ˋfulˌflɛdʒd] *adj.* 有充分資格的

留學　超實用單字

CD 2-25

Clubs and Socializing 社團與社交

★ **sports club** [`sports ˌklʌb] *n.* 體育社

> Friend: Want to join the basketball sports club? It's not an official school team, but you still get to play against other schools.
> You: Sure. I used to play on a team back home.

> 朋友： 想不想加入籃球體育社？籃球社不是正式的校隊，但是你還是有機會和其他學校對打。
> 你： 好啊，我以前在老家也是籃球隊的。

★ **fine arts organization** [`faɪn `ɑrts ɔrgənəˌzeʃən] *n.* 藝術社團

> Friend: There are a lot of fine arts organizations here.
> You: Yeah, there are over twenty singing groups[1] and ten theater organizations.[2]

> 朋友： 這裡有很多藝術社團。
> 你： 是啊，有 20 多個合唱團和 10 個戲劇社。

★ **retreat** [rɪ`trit] *n.* 靜休會

> You: All the CSA[3] officers are going on a retreat this weekend.
> Friend: That's good. You guys can bond[4] and really get to know each other.

> 你： 這週末中國同學會的所有幹部都要參加靜修會。
> 朋友： 很好啊，你們可以團結在一起，真正互相了解。

[Word List]

1. singing group [`sɪŋɪŋ ˌgrup] *n.* 合唱團
2. theater organization [`θiətɚ ɔrgənəˌzeʃən] *n.* 戲劇社
3. CSA (=Chinese Student Association) 中國同學會
4. bond [bɑnd] *v.* 結合；團結在一起

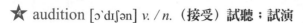

★ audition [ɔ`dɪʃən] v. / n.（接受）試聽；試演

Friend: Are you auditioning for an a cappella group?[1]
You: Yup. My audition is next Tuesday.

朋友： 你是不是要去接受一個無伴奏合唱團的試聽?
你： 是啊，我的試聽是下禮拜二。

★ tryout [`traɪ,aut] n. 甄試；選拔賽

You: I'm thinking of joining the debating society.[2]
Friend: There are tryouts this Friday. You have to give a 5-minute speech.

你： 我在考慮加入辯論社。
朋友： 這禮拜五有選拔賽。你得準備個五分鐘的演講。

Rush Week 新生招收週

★ big sis [`bɪg`sɪs] n. 大姊

You: Now that you're pledging, do you have a "big sister?"
Friend: I sure do! My big sis is great. She buys me gifts, takes me out to dinner, and even arranged for an a cappella group to give me a private concert!

妳： 既然都要宣誓了，妳有「大姊」嗎？
朋友： 當然有啊！我的大姊很棒！她買禮物給我、帶我出去吃飯，甚至還安排了無伴奏合唱團為我表演一場私人的演奏會！

[Word List]

1. a cappella group [ɑ kə`pɛlə ,grup] n.
無伴奏之合聲合唱團（a cappella 為義大利文）

2. debating society [dɪ`betɪŋ sə,saɪətɪ] n.
辯論社

CD 2-26

⭐ multicultural interest sorority [ˌmʌltɪˈkʌltʃərəl ˈɪntrɪst səˌrɔrətɪ] *n.* 多文化關懷姊妹會

You:　　I don't think I want to join a sorority.

Friend:　What about a multicultural interest sorority? They have all the ideals of a traditional sorority, but you get to meet people of all races[1] and backgrounds.

你：　　我不認為我想加入姊妹會。

朋友：　加入多文化關懷姊妹會如何？她們具備有傳統姊妹會所有的理念，但可以認識各種不同種族和背景的人。

⭐ charter [ˈtʃɑrtɚ] *n.* 特許狀

Friend:　We're starting the first Asian[2] American fraternity here!

You:　　When do you become an actual charter of the fraternity?

朋友：　我們要在這裡成立第一個亞裔美人兄弟會！

你：　　你們什麼時候會獲得兄弟會的特許狀？

⭐ chapter [ˈtʃæptɚ] *n.* 分會；支部

You:　　We've just received chapter status from our national sorority council.[3]

Friend:　Congratulations! Your sorority has really grown in the last three years.

你：　　我們剛從國際姊妹協會收到分會資格。

朋友：　恭喜！妳們的姊妹會三年來真的成長不少。

[Word List]

1. race [res] *n.* 種族；民族

2. Asian [ˈeʒən] *adj.* 亞洲的

3. council [ˈkaʊnsl̩] *n.* 協商會；政務會

☆ **pledge class** [`plɛdʒ ˌklæs] *n.* **宣誓級**

Friend: We're choosing our Beta[1] pledge class tonight.
You: Since you founded the sorority, does that mean your class was the Alpha[2] class?

朋友： 今天晚上我們要選出貝塔屆的宣誓成員。
你： 既然這個姊妹會是妳創立的，這是不是表示妳是阿法屆的？

☆ **inter-fraternity / inter-sorority council** [ɪn`tɚ frə`tɚnətɪ / ɪn`tɚ sə`rorətɪ `kaʊnsḷ] *n.* **相互兄弟 / 相互姊妹協會**

You: What's the inter-fraternity council?
Friend: It's the governing body of all the social fraternities.

你： 什麼是相互兄弟協會？
朋友： 它是所有社交兄弟會的指導團體。

[Word List]

1. Beta [`betə] *n.* 希臘文的第二個字母      2. Alpha [`ælfə] *n.* 希臘文的第一個字母

留學 佈告欄

Taiwanese Student Association
1st General Meeting

Find out what TSA is all about at our 1st general meeting of the year! We'll talk about what events are coming up and how you can get involved. Free dessert provided!

Wednesday, 8th Sep.
7:30 p.m.
South Meeting Room

[翻　譯]

台灣同學會
第一次會員大會

　　請來參加我們今年第一次的會員大會,瞧瞧台灣同學會到底是什麼碗糕!我們將討論即將舉辦的活動以及你要如何才能加入。免費提供甜點!

九月八號禮拜三

晚上七點半

南邊會議室

留學 智慧王

The Greek System 希臘系統

「希臘系統」，或稱為「希臘生活」、「希臘社群」，指的便是大學內的兄弟會和姊妹會。這些團體以希臘字母命名，故稱希臘系統，推廣兄弟／姊妹情誼、社區精神、學術成就和領導技巧。這些團體歷史悠久，並擁有自己獨特的傳統（第一個大學兄弟會便成立於 1776 年！）；許多兄弟會在美國各地均設有分會。身為兄弟會或姊妹會的一員，即使在你大學畢業後，仍會有很多好處。由於一旦加入後便被視為終身會員，在找工作時都有可能得到「兄弟」或「姊妹」的協助！

希臘組織很活躍，校園內的派對也多由兄弟會舉辦。有的還可能擁有專屬的會館供會員居住。希臘組織的會費不便宜，你可能得繳交入會費（initiation fee）、會勳費（pin fee）和其他相關費用。

Cultural Organizations 文化組織

文化組織通常會舉辦表演、籌備活動及從事社區教育以推廣不同的文化。加入學校的台灣或中國同學會可以認識其他台灣來的學生。搬家安頓時如遇到困難，找這類組織幫忙準沒錯。許多文化組織會幫助外籍學生搬家並認識新朋友。不過不要光顧著認識台灣人，要記得多參加校內的其他活動，充分豐富你的留學經驗。

Community Service Activities 社區服務活動

許多學生對社區服務很有興趣。你可以參加學校的各類組織，從事義工活動。最受歡迎的組織包括：

★ 人道安家組織（Habitat for Humanity）
為一國際性的非營利組織，專門幫助低收入戶解決住家問題。安家義工和

安家住戶攜手合作，稱之為「合夥家庭」。合夥家庭必須付出幾百小時的人力（「以汗水換房子」），幫自己和其他合夥家庭蓋房子。由於不必給付蓋房子的工資和利息，住安家屋費用相當低廉。

★ 舞蹈馬拉松（Dance Marathon）

這是一個 24 小時的募款會，許多大學都會舉辦。參加的人必須連續跳 24 小時的舞（至少得站著，不能坐下），不得間斷。

★ 四分之一協會（One-in-Four）

是一個性侵害同儕教育團體，會員均為男性。這個組織專門教導男性認識強暴，並指導他們如何幫助女性走出性侵害的陰影。

Sports 體育

大學代表隊是正式的校隊，但由於大部分的學生沒機會參加，校內還有其他各種社團可供選擇。社團體育隊可以參加校外比賽，和其他大學的體育性社團對打。校內體育競賽則純粹是娛樂性質，任何組織都可以參與。

Student Government 學生政府

每所大學都設有學生政府，成員包括學生和教職員代表，學生政府由學生組成，每年會由二年級或三年級等選出當屆主席。這些代表人員的主要目標在於解決學生的切身問題，並與學校合作，共同改善學生的生活。

Other Organizations 其他組織

喜歡唱歌、跳舞、演戲和畫畫的人，學校都會有適合的社團。同樣地，如果你愛打線上遊戲、認為應該提升女性對數學和科學的興趣，或者你想做校園

導覽人員，校內也有這類社團可以參加。有的社團的競爭激烈（得參加試聽會、選拔賽或透過申請程序），有的則照單全收。不管怎麼說，請踴躍參加，享受社團樂趣！

List of Student Organizations 學生組織名單

Arab Student Organization [`ærəb `stjudṇt ˌɔrgənəˋzeʃən]	n. 阿拉伯同學會
Baha'i Faith Group [bəˋhaɪ ˋfeθ ˌgrup]	n. 巴海信仰團體
Chinese Student Association [tʃarˋniz ˋstjudṇt əˌsosɪˋeʃən]	n. 中國同學會
Dance Club [ˋdæns ˌklʌb]	n. 舞蹈社
Engineering Students Council [ˌɛndʒəˋnɪrɪŋ ˋstjudṇts ˋkaʊnsḷ]	n. 工程學生諮委會
Filmmakers Organization [ˋfɪlmˌmekəˑz ˌɔrgənəˋzeʃən]	n. 電影人組織協會
Golden Key Honor Society [ˋgoldṇ ˋki ˋanəˑ səˌsaɪətɪ]	n. 金鑰匙榮譽協會
Habitat for Humanity [ˋhæbəˌtæt fɔr hjuˋmænətɪ]	n. 人道安家組織
Indian Student Association [ˋɪndɪən ˋstjudṇt əˌsosɪˋeʃən]	n. 印度同學會
Jewish Student Group [ˋdʒuɪʃ ˋstjudṇt ˋgrup]	n. 猶太學生團體
Kappa Delta Sorority [ˋkæpə ˋdɛltə səˋrɔrətɪ]	n. Kappa Delta 姊妹會
Latino Student Union [ləˋtino ˋstjudṇt ˋjunjən]	n. 拉丁學生聯盟
Multiracial Student Union [mʌltaɪˋreʃəl ˋstjudṇt ˋjunjən]	n. 多種族學生聯盟
National Society of Collegiate Scholars [ˋnæʃənḷ səˋsaɪətɪ əv kəˋlidʒɪɪt ˋskaləˑz]	
	n. 國立學院學者協會
Pakistan Student Association [ˌpækɪˋstæn ˋstjudṇt əˌsosɪˋeʃən]	n. 巴基斯坦同學會
Queer Student Union [ˋkwɪr ˋstjudṇt ˋjunjən]	n. 同性戀學生聯盟
Red Cross Club [ˋrɛd ˋkrɔs ˌklʌb]	n. 紅十字社
Sailing Club [ˋselɪŋ ˌklʌb]	n. 風帆社
Tae Kwon Do Club [ˋtaɪ ˋkwanˋdo ˌklʌb]	n. 跆拳道社
University Democrats [ˌjunəˋvɝsətɪ ˋdɛməˌkræts]	n. 大學民主社
Vietnamese Student Association [ˌvjɛtnəˋmiz ˋstjudṇt əˌsosɪˋeʃən]	
	n. 越南同學會
Women's Ice Hockey [ˋwɪmənz ˋaɪs ˌhakɪ]	n. 女子冰上曲棍球隊
Young Life Leadership [ˋjʌŋ ˋlaɪf ˋlidəˑˌʃɪp]	n. 青年生命領導社

Chapter 11

Partying the Night Away

派對鬧通宵

Get out and party!

What would a university experience be without parties? While most on-campus parties tend to be held in fraternity houses, organizations and clubs will also hold parties. Celebrating your 21st birthday is one of the highlights for undergraduate students, as the legal drinking age in American is twenty-one. Graduate students will usually go out for a drink with friends, or hold parties in their houses or apartments.

外出狂歡去！

沒參加過派對怎麼算唸過大學？雖然大部分的校內派對多半是在兄弟會的會館內舉行，但組織和社團也會辦派對。對大學部學生而言，慶祝 21 歲的生日是一大盛事，因為在美國，飲酒的合法年齡是 21 歲。研究生則通常會和朋友出去喝酒，或在自己家或公寓裡辦派對。

TOP 10 必會字彙

CD 2-28

★ mixer
['mɪksɚ]
n. 聯誼會

② costume party
['kastum ˌpɑrtɪ]
n. 化妝舞會

★ decoration
[ˌdɛkə`reʃən]
n. 佈置;裝飾品

★ formal
['fɔrml̩]
n.(須穿晚禮服的)正式舞會

⑤ ball
[bɔl]
n. 舞會

⑥ potluck
['pɑt`lʌk]
n. 家常餐會(每人帶一道菜參加)

★ blender
['blɛndɚ]
n. 果汁機;做菜用的攪拌器

★ cocktail
['kak,tel]
n. 雞尾酒

⑨ cocktail shaker
['kak,tel ˌʃekɚ]
n. 雞尾酒調製器

⑩ ice bucket
['aɪs ˌbʌkɪt]
n. 冰桶

CD 2-29

1 A: The CSA is having a mixer on Saturday with the KSA.

B: I know. It's going to be a costume party. What are you going as?

A: 星期六中國同學會要和韓國同學會舉辦聯誼。

B: 我知道。那將是一場化妝舞會。你要打扮成什麼去？

---

2 A: The decorations at the formal last night were really beautiful.

B: Yeah, but you should have seen the ones at our ball.

A: 昨晚那場正式舞會的佈置真的很漂亮。

B: 是啊，不過你該瞧瞧我們舞會的佈置的。

---

3 A: What should I bring to your potluck on Friday?

B: Salad and bread. Oh yeah, bring your blender for drinks.

A: 星期五我該帶什麼食物參加你的家常餐會？

B: 沙拉和麵包。哦，對了，把你的果汁機帶來好做喝的。

---

4 A: Let's have a cocktail party.

B: All right. I have a cocktail shaker, but we'll have to get an ice bucket.

A: 咱們辦場雞尾酒派對吧。

B: 好。我有一個雞尾酒調製器，不過我們得去買個冰桶。

你可以跟我這樣說

CD **2-30**

Dialogue A

Annie goes to Zach's 21ˢᵗ birthday party.

Annie: Hey Zach. Happy Birthday!

Zach: Thanks, Annie. I'm glad you can make it. Can I get you a drink?

Annie: Sure. What do you have?

Zach: There are beers in that cooler, but we also have a keg of really good German beer in the kitchen. We've also got wine, and a bunch of stuff to make mixed drinks in the kitchen. And of course we've got soda and fruit juice if you don't want any alcohol.

Annie: You're such a great host! I'll try some of that German beer. But you might have to help me with the tap. I never get anything but foam.

Zach: Ha ... sure, no problem. You up for beer pong? They're playing it in the back.

Annie: What is beer pong?

Zach: You have two teams and place six cups of beer on each end of the ping-pong table. You have to bounce or throw a ping-pong ball into a cup at the opposite end. If you get it in, the person from the other team has to drink the beer.

Annie: Umm ... maybe I'll watch a few games first! Or let me teach you some Chinese drinking games!

Zach: Hey, now that sounds cool.

Annie: OK, help me with the tap, and I'll teach you the first game. It's called five, ten, fifteen. You start with two people and ...

安妮參加札克21歲的慶生會。

安妮：嘿，札克。生日快樂！

札克：謝啦，安妮。很高興妳能來。要不要拿杯飲料給妳？

安妮：好啊。你有什麼？

札克：冷藏箱裡有啤酒，不過我們廚房也有一桶很棒的德國啤酒。我們也供應
　　　葡萄酒，廚房裡還有一堆可以做雞尾酒的東西。如果妳不想喝酒的話，
　　　我們當然也準備了汽水和果汁。

安妮：你真是個好主人！我就來點德國啤酒吧。不過你可能得幫我開拴塞。每
　　　次除了泡沫，我什麼都沒裝到。

札克：哈……當然，沒問題。想不想玩啤酒乒乓？他們正在後面那邊玩。

安妮：什麼叫啤酒乒乓？

札克：就是分兩隊，然後在乒乓球桌的兩端各放六杯啤酒。妳必須把乒乓球彈
　　　進或丟進對面的杯子中。如果進了，對手隊其中一人就必須喝那杯啤
　　　酒。

安妮：嗯……或許我先觀看幾局吧！還是就讓我教你們幾個中式喝酒遊戲！

札克：嘿，聽起來挺酷的。

安妮：好，幫我開拴塞，我教你第一個遊戲。這遊戲叫做五、十、十五。要有
　　　兩個人，然後……

[Words & Phrases]

- cooler [`kulɚ] *n.* 冷藏箱
- keg [kɛg] *n.* 小木桶；啤酒桶
- a bunch of 一大堆
- mixed drink [`mɪkst `drɪŋk] *n.* 調酒；
  雞尾酒
- tap [tæp] *n.* （酒桶等的）塞子；栓子
- foam [fom] *n.* 泡沫
- beer pong [`bɪr ˌpaŋ] *n.* 啤酒乒乓
- drinking game [`drɪŋkɪŋ ˌgem] *n.* 喝酒
  遊戲

你可以跟我這樣說

 CD 2-31

Dialogue B

Kevin goes out for a beer with a few friends.

Waitress: What can I get for you tonight?

Kevin: I'll take a Guinness.

Brian: I'll have a Budweiser.

Waitress: We only have that in bottles right now. Is that okay?

Brian: Hmm. What else do you have on tap?

Waitress: Sam Adams, Pilsner Urquell, Bass, and Harp.

Brian: In that case, I'll have a black and tan.

Christine: And I'll have a strawberry daiquiri, please.

Waitress: No problem. I'll just need to see some I.D. first.

Kevin: I suppose we should take it as a compliment that we don't look like we're over twenty-one!

Waitress: Nah, it's just our boss's rules. *(They show him their I.D.s)* Thanks. I'll be right back with your drinks.

Brian: Hey, check out that girl over there. She looks totally trashed.

Kevin: She's wasted!

Christine: She looks like she's about to throw up. Her friends better get her out of here before she heaves all over the bar.

Kevin: I'm always surprised about how much American students drink.

Brian: You think that's bad? You should go to a frat party!

Christine: Totally. They're just drink-a-thons! Just a few beers with friends is the way to go.

Kevin: I'll drink to that.

All: Cheers!

凱文和幾個朋友出去喝啤酒。

服務生： 請問各位今晚想點些什麼？

凱文： 我要點健力士黑啤酒。

布萊恩： 我要百威啤酒。

服務生： 我們現在只有瓶裝的百威，可以嗎？

布萊恩： 嗯。那你們有什麼是桶裝的？

服務生： 山姆亞當斯、皮爾森、巴斯和哈普。

布萊恩： 這樣的話，我來杯黑啤跟淡啤混合酒。

克莉絲汀：那我要草莓代基里酒，麻煩你。

服務生： 沒問題，不過我需要先看一下各位的證件。

凱文： 我想我們應該把這視為是一種恭維，我們看起來不像滿 21 歲！

服務生： 才不是呢，這不過是我們老闆的規定罷了。（他們把證件拿給服務
生看。）謝了。我馬上回來幫你們上飲料。

布萊恩： 嘿，瞧那邊那個女生，她看起來醉得一塌糊塗。

凱文： 她是醉到不行！

克莉絲汀：她看起來快吐了。她的朋友最好在她把酒吧吐得到處都是之前，帶
她離開。

凱文： 我對美國學生這麼能喝總覺得很驚訝。

布萊恩： 你認為這很糟嗎？那你該到兄弟會派對去瞧瞧！

克莉絲汀：完全沒錯。他們真是喝不停！跟朋友小喝幾杯啤酒才叫上道。

凱文： 我為這一點乾一杯。

大家： 乾杯！

[Words & Phrases]

- Guinness [ˋgɪnɪs] n.【商標】健力士黑啤酒（愛爾蘭）
- Budweiser [ˋbʌdˌwaɪzɚ] n.【商標】百威啤酒（美國）
- on tap 桶裝的
- Sam Adams [ˋsæm ˋædəmz] n.【商標】山姆亞當斯啤酒（美國）
- Pilsner Urquell [ˋpɪlznɚ ˋɝkwel] n.【商標】皮爾森啤酒（捷克）
- Bass [bes] n.【商標】巴斯啤酒（英國）
- Harp [hɑrp] n.【商標】哈普啤酒（愛爾蘭）
- daiquiri [ˋdaɪkərɪ] n.（調酒）代基里酒
- trashed [træʃt] adj. 爛醉的
- wasted [ˋwestɪd] adj.（俚）醉到不行的
- throw up 嘔吐
- heave [hiv] v. 嘔吐
- frat [fræt] n. 兄弟會（fraternity 的簡稱）
- drink-a-thons 馬拉松（marathon）式地喝
- the way to go 正途

留學　超實用單字

CD 2-32

Parties and Socials 派對與社交活動

★ semi-formal [ˌsɛmɪˈfɔrml̩] *n.* 半正式舞會

You:　What do you wear to a semi-formal?
Friend:　Most girls usually wear a short formal dress. Guys just need to go in a suit.

你：　　參加半正式舞會要穿什麼？
朋友：　大部分的女生會穿正式短洋裝。男生只需穿西裝參加就可以了。

❷ bartender [ˈbarˌtɛndɚ] *n.* 酒保

You:　I can't order our drinks. The bartender won't pay attention to me.
Friend:　There are too many people around the bar. Wave some money at him and he'll come over.

你：　　我點不到飲料。酒保不理我。
朋友：　酒吧裡人太多了。用鈔票向他揮一揮，他就會過來了。

❸ cover charge [ˈkʌvɚ ˌtʃardʒ] *n.* 服務費

You:　Do we have to pay to go to the party?
Friend:　There's a $10 cover charge.

你：　　參加派對要不要付費？
朋友：　要付 10 美元的服務費。

Making Drinks 調飲料

★ liquor [ˋlɪkɚ] *n.* **烈酒;酒精飲料**

You: I get a headache whenever I drink hard[1] liquor. I'd better stick to[2] wine.

Friend: How about beer?

你: 每次喝烈酒我就頭痛。我最好還是喝葡萄酒就好。

朋友: 那啤酒呢?

★ shot [ʃɑt] *n.* **小杯烈酒**

Friend: What's that shot Steph's drinking?

You: I think it's called a Lemon Drop[3]. It's really sweet.

朋友: 史帝夫喝的那一小杯烈酒是什麼?

你: 好像叫做檸檬糖。非常甜。

★ chaser [ˋtʃesɚ] *n.* **飲烈酒後喝的飲料(水、啤酒等)**

Friend: Yuck. That shot was so strong.

You: Here, drink some coke as a chaser.

朋友: 嗯。那一小杯烈酒好強勁。

你: 來,喝些可樂,當作酒後飲料。

[Word List]

1. hard [hɑrd] *adj.* 含酒精成分多的;烈性的

2. stick to 固守;堅持

3. Lemon Drop [ˋlɛmən ˌdrɑp] *n.* 檸檬糖(一種調酒,由伏特加、檸檬汁和糖調成)

CD 2-33

★ strainer [`strenɚ] *n.* **過濾器**

Friend: You put ice cubes[1] in the shaker, shake, and then pour[2] out the drink.

You: We'll need to use a strainer to make sure the ice cubes don't get poured out as well.

朋友： 把冰塊放進調酒器，搖一搖，然後把飲料倒出來。

你： 我們得用過濾器，以免冰塊也一起倒出來。

★ corkscrew [`kɔrk͵skru] *n.* **軟木塞開瓶器**

You: Want a glass of wine?

Friend: Sure. But I think we lost our corkscrew.

你： 要不要來杯葡萄酒？

朋友： 好啊。但我們的開瓶器好像搞丟了。

★ bottle opener [`batl͵opənɚ] *n.* **啤酒開瓶器**

Friend: Don't open your beer with your teeth!

You: I'm too lazy to get a bottle opener.

朋友： 不要用牙齒開啤酒！

你： 我懶得去拿開瓶器。

[Word List]

1. ice cube [`aɪs͵kjub] *n.* 冰塊

2. pour [por] *v.* 倒；注入

178

★ garnish [`gɑrnɪʃ] *v.* 裝飾;添加配菜於……

Friend: You're supposed to garnish the drink with a slice of pineapple[1].
You: I'll add a cherry as well.

朋友: 你應該要用一片鳳梨來裝飾這飲料。
你: 我也加一顆櫻桃好了。

★ swizzle stick [`swɪzḷ ˏstɪk] *n.* 調酒棒

You: OK, here's the olive[2] for this cocktail. Now what do I do with it?
Friend: Put it on the swizzle stick and then put it in the drink.

你: 好這是雞尾酒需要的橄欖。現在我要怎麼做?
朋友: 把它放在調酒棒上,然後再把它放進飲料中。

[**Word List**]

1. pineapple [`paɪnˏæpḷ] *n.* 鳳梨;菠蘿        2. olive [`ɑlɪv] *n.* 橄欖

留學 佈告欄

You're invited to ...

Zach' 21st Birthday Bash[1]!

★ When: Friday, February 4th, 2005 8 p.m.
★ Where: Apt# 3, 116 15th Street
★ Tel: (592) 273-5839

The party will move to Club K downtown at 11 p.m.

[翻　譯]

敬邀您參加……

札克的 21 歲慶生會！

日期：2005 年 2 月 4 號星期五晚上 8 點
地點：第 15 街 116 號，三號公寓
電話：(592) 273-5839

晚上 11 點派對將轉移到市中心的 K 俱樂部

[Word List]

・bash [bæʃ] *n.* （口語）宴會；派對

留學 智慧王

Throw a Party 辦派對

派對的規模不一，小自一小群朋友聚在一起喝喝啤酒，大至有現場樂隊（live band）和外燴食物（catered food）。派對用品店中應有盡有，裝飾品、戲服、邀請函甚至各種塑膠杯，都買得到。要辦個成功的派對，一點都不用愁。

一些派對點子：

★ 化妝舞會（Costume party）

每名來賓穿戲服盛裝出席派對。你可以設定主題，例如「故事書中的人物」或「名人」。

★ 雞尾酒夜（Cocktail night）

選擇一種雞尾酒，提供不同的口味，例如不同口味的馬丁尼（傳統、蘋果、荔枝等）。

★ 家常餐會（Potluck）

每個人帶一道菜來跟大家分享。這種聚會可以減輕主人需要準備很多食物的壓力。

★ 車尾派對（Tailgating）

車尾派對是球賽前舉辦的烤肉會或派對。這類聚會有時在球場的停車場中舉辦，或在球場附近的住家舉辦。

★ 壽司夜（Sushi night）

邀請眾多好友一起學做壽司。不會做壽司也沒關係。上網找資料，購買好所有食材，邊學邊做最好玩！

Drinking Games 喝酒遊戲

喝酒遊戲在美國的大學生中非常流行。除了啤酒乒乓外，還有很多其他種類的喝酒遊戲（有的和台灣玩的遊戲很類似）。以下提供一些常見的喝酒遊戲：

★ 二毛五（Quarters）

這個遊戲和啤酒乒乓有異曲同工之妙。每個人用二毛五硬幣，想辦法讓它從桌上彈進玻璃杯中。彈進了，對手就必須喝酒。請在遊戲開始之前決定好規則。

★ 說真話、接受挑戰或喝酒！（Truth, Dare, or Drink!）

第一個玩的人先問左手邊的人一個問題，可問私人問題，或其他任何問題。被問的人可以回答問題、接受挑戰或選擇喝酒。陷阱就在於是由提問的人指定該喝哪一種酒。如果對方選擇接受挑戰，提問的人就要選擇挑戰種類。要是拒絕接受挑戰，被問的人就必須喝兩倍的酒。回答問題，或喝了酒之後，被問的人可以在一群人中任選一人，問下一個問題。如此重複下去，想玩多久就玩多久！

★ 我從來沒有……（I Never ...）

這個遊戲從一個人先說「我從來沒有……」開始玩。這個人說出一件從來沒有做過的事情。如能發揮創意，遊戲會比較好玩。做過那件事情的人必須喝酒。你會發現大家做過哪些意想不到的事情。如果有人不承認自己做過某件事，但是有人知道那個人做過這件事，那個人還是得喝酒。

How To Mix Drinks 如何調酒

以下提供最普遍調製雞尾酒的材料，另附加幾種最有名雞尾酒的調配方式：

Liquors 烈酒

CD **2-34**

• vodka [ˈvɑdkə]	n. 伏特加
• gin [ʤɪn]	n. 琴酒
• rum [rʌm]	n. 蘭姆酒

- tequila [tə`kilə]　　　　　　　　　　*n.* 龍舌蘭酒
- scotch [skɑtʃ]　　　　　　　　　　　*n.* 蘇格蘭威士忌酒
- brandy [`brændɪ]　　　　　　　　　*n.* 白蘭地
- vermouth [vɚ`muθ]　　　　　　　　*n.* 苦艾酒
- triple sec [`trɪpḷ ˌsɛk]　　　　　　*n.* 白橙皮酒

Garnishes 裝飾
CD **2-35**

- orange [`ɔrəndʒ]　　　　　　　　　*n.* 柳丁
- lemon [`lɛmən]　　　　　　　　　　*n.* 檸檬
- pineapple [`paɪnˌæpḷ]　　　　　　*n.* 鳳梨
- apple [`æpḷ]　　　　　　　　　　　*n.* 蘋果
- maraschino cherry [ˌmærə`skino ˌtʃɛrɪ]　*n.* 調味櫻桃
- mint [mɪnt]　　　　　　　　　　　*n.* 薄荷
- olive [`ɑlɪv]　　　　　　　　　　　*n.* 橄欖

Glasses 杯子
CD **2-36**

- shot glass [`ʃɑt ˌglæs]　　　　　　*n.* 小烈酒杯
- tumbler [`tʌmblɚ]　　　　　　　　*n.* 平底無腳酒杯
- martini glass [mɑr`tini ˌglæs]　　*n.* 馬丁尼杯
- wine glass [`waɪn ˌglæs]　　　　　*n.* 葡萄酒杯
- champagne glass [ʃæm`pen ˌglæs]　*n.* 香檳杯
- beer mug [`bɪr ˌmʌg]　　　　　　　*n.* 啤酒杯
- pilsner glass [`pɪlznɚ ˌglæs]　　　*n.* 喝啤酒用的細長玻璃杯
- highball glass [`haɪˌbɔl ˌglæs]　　*n.* 高球杯
- Collins glass [`kɑlɪnz ˌglæs]　　　*n.* 柯林斯杯

Cocktails 雞尾酒

★**Martini** [mar`tinɪ] *n.* 馬丁尼

琴酒	1 又 1/2 盎司
無甜味苦艾酒	3/4 盎司
橄欖	一顆

調酒杯中放入冰塊，倒入琴酒和苦艾酒後攪拌。用過濾器將飲料倒入雞尾酒杯中，放進橄欖後即可飲用。

★**Cosmopolitan** [ˌkɑzmə`palətn̩] *n.* 柯夢波丹

伏特加	1 盎司
白橙皮酒	1/2 盎司
蘿絲甜萊姆汁	1/2 盎司
蔓越梅汁	1/2 盎司
萊姆鍥形切片	

將液體材料和冰塊放入調酒器，搖一搖。完成後在杯緣上放一片萊姆切片，即可享用！

★**Frozen Daiquiri** [`frozn̩ `daɪkərɪ] *n.* 冰代基里酒

淡蘭姆酒	1 又 1/2 盎司
白橙皮酒	1 湯匙
蘭姆汁	1 又 1/2 盎司
糖	1 茶匙
櫻桃	1 顆
碎冰塊	1 杯

將所有的材料（櫻桃除外）放入電動果汁機，以低速攪拌五秒鐘，然後以高速攪拌直到材料變堅實。將材料倒入代基里杯，放上櫻桃後即可飲用。

★Margarita [ˌmɑrgəˋritə] *n.* 瑪格莉特

龍舌蘭酒	1 又 1/2 盎司
白橙皮酒	1/2 盎司
萊姆汁	1 盎司
鹽	

在雞尾酒杯的杯緣抹上萊姆汁，杯緣沾上鹽。將所有材料連同冰塊一起搖好，然後用過濾器倒入沾了鹽的杯子中即可飲用。

Nursing the Hangover 宿醉的處理

好了，你昨天在派對中瘋了一整晚，連自己怎麼回到家的都不知道，現在起床了，頭痛欲裂。這時該怎麼辦呢？剛起床絕對不可能一下消除宿醉的感覺，不過可以試一試以下的家庭療法，讓自己覺得好過一些。

宿醉療法：
★ 蜂蜜──塗在土司上食用。蜂蜜中的果糖可以加快身體消化酒精的速度。
★ 蕃茄汁──另一個攝取果糖的好方法。
★ 咖啡因──喝咖啡可以振奮你的精神，放鬆造成頭痛的腦血管，有助於改善宿醉的症狀。

下次該如何避免宿醉：
★ 喝酒的當晚務必喝大量的水。
★ 不要混著喝太多的酒精飲料。比方，不要喝了葡萄酒後又喝螺絲起子，之後又喝啤酒！
★ 可服用特殊的解酒藥，避免宿醉。解酒藥並不會妨礙感受酒精的效力。
★ 切記不要空腹喝酒。

Chapter 12

Holidays! Celebrate!
假日到了！慶祝一番吧！

American holidays

If you study abroad in the United States, rest assured you'll have some days off from school. In addition to Christmas and New Year's Day, Americans enjoy several federal holidays. Many of them fall on Mondays to give students, workers, and families a three-day holiday. Some of these holidays include Président's Day (3rd Monday in February), Memorial Day (last Monday in May), and Columbus Day (2nd Monday in October). And of course there is the very American holiday of Thanksgiving. It always begins on the 4th Thursday of November and includes Friday, giving everyone a four-day break to enjoy some traditional festivities.

美國假日

如果你是到美國留學，請放心，一定會有幾天可以不用上課。除了聖誕節和新年外，美國人還有好幾個國定假日。許多假日都訂在星期一，以便讓學生、上班族和家庭可以享受連續三天的假期。這些假日包括總統日（二月的第三個星期一）、陣亡將士紀念日（五月的最後一個星期一）和哥倫布日（十月的第二個星期一）。另外當然還有非常美國的感恩節。感恩節假期從十一月的第四個星期四開始，包括星期五在內，讓大家有四天的連假歡度傳統的節慶。

Top 10 必會字彙

 CD **2-37**

★ **Spring Break** [`sprɪŋ ˌbrek]		*n.* 春假
★ **dive** [daɪv]		*v.* 潛水
★ **snorkeling** [`snɔrklɪŋ]		*n.* 浮潛
★ **bikini** [bɪ`kinɪ]		*n.* 比基尼
★ **board shorts** [`bord ˌʃɔrts]		*n.* 及膝泳褲
★ **Speedo** [`spiˌdo]		*n.* 三角緊身泳褲
★ **Winter Break** [`wɪntɚ ˌbrek]		*n.* 寒假
★ **water ski** [`wɔtɚ ˌski]		*v.* 滑水
★ **snow ski** [`sno ˌski]		*v.* 滑雪
★ **Thanksgiving** [`θæŋksˌgɪvɪŋ]		*n.* 感恩節

CD **2-38**

1 A: Spring Break is coming up! You have any plans?

B: Yep. I'm going to go diving. It should be cooler than snorkeling.

A: 春假快到了！你有沒有什麼計畫？

B: 有啊。我要去潛水。潛水應該比浮潛酷。

---

2 A: Hey, I see you bought a new bikini. Can I go to the beach with you?

B: Yes, if you promise to wear board shorts, and not that Speedo.

A: 嘿，看來妳買了件新的比基尼。我可以和妳一起去海邊嗎？

B: 可以，但你得答應穿及膝泳褲，不能穿那條三角緊身泳褲。

---

3 A: For Winter Break, I'm going to Florida to water ski.

B: Sounds fun. I'm going snow skiing in Washington.

A: 寒假的時候，我要去佛羅里達州滑水。

B: 聽起來很好玩。我要去華盛頓滑雪。

---

4 A: What are your plans for Thanksgiving?

B: I'm going to a friend's for dinner. And I'm going to catch up on some reading!

A: 你感恩節有什麼計畫？

B: 我要去朋友家吃晚餐。我還想趕一下閱讀進度！

你可以跟我這樣說

CD 2-39

Dialogue A

Kevin spends Thanksgiving with Brian's family.

Kevin:	Thanks for having me over for Thanksgiving.
Brian:	No problem. My parents are glad you can spend the holidays with us. Have you ever had Thanksgiving dinner before?
Kevin:	Nope. But I know you eat turkey.
Brian:	That's a given. Plus mashed potatoes and pumpkin pie!
Kevin:	What's Thanksgiving about, anyway?
Brian:	Well, a group of settlers from England, called the Pilgrims, came to America to escape religious persecution. Many of them died during their first winter here. The Native Americans taught the Pilgrims how to grow corn and other crops, so they were able to survive the next winter. The Pilgrims then invited the Native Americans to a thanksgiving feast, to thank them for all their help.
Mrs. Kestner:	Brian, can you put the stuffing and biscuits on the table, please?
Brian:	Sure, mom.
Kevin:	Wait a second. What's stuffing? I've heard about it, but I don't know what it is. And those don't look like biscuits.
Brian:	It's made from breadcrumbs and spices and then stuffed into the turkey before the bird is roasted. And these *(picking one up)* are southern biscuits. They're a little like bread rolls. They're one of my mom's specialties. Well, dinner's almost on. What are you thankful for?
Kevin:	I'm definitely thankful for this incredible meal we're going to have! And of course, the chance I have to study here.

凱文和布萊恩的家人一起過感恩節。

凱文： 謝謝你邀請我到你們家過感恩節。

布萊恩： 別客氣。我爸媽很高興你能和我們一起過節。你之前有沒有吃過感恩節晚餐？

凱文： 沒有，不過我知道你們會吃火雞。

布萊恩： 那個大家都知道。還會有馬鈴薯泥和南瓜派！

凱文： 那，感恩節到底是怎麼一回事？

布萊恩： 嗯，一群來自英國的移民，叫做清教徒，為了逃離宗教迫害來到了美國。其中有很多人在這裡的第一個冬天就死了。美國原住民教這些清教徒如何種玉米和其他農作物，他們才得以撐過下一個冬天。於是這些清教徒便邀請美國原住民吃感恩盛宴，謝謝他們所做的一切協助。

凱斯納太太： 布萊恩，可不可以請你把火雞餡和比司吉放到桌上。

布萊恩： 好的，媽。

凱文： 等一下，火雞餡是什麼？我聽說過，但是不知道那是啥。而那些看起來也不像餅乾。

布萊恩： 這餡是用麵包屑和香料做成的，在烘烤火雞前塞進它的肚子裡。而這些 *(拿起一個)* 則是南方比司吉，有一點像麵包捲。它們可是我媽的私房菜之一。嗯，晚餐快上桌了。你要感謝什麼？

凱文： 我一定要對這頓我們即將要吃的大餐表示感謝！此外當然還要感謝能有機會到這兒唸書。

[Words & Phrases]

- given [ˋgɪvən] *n.* 眾所皆知的事
- mashed potato [ˋmæʃt pəˋteto] *n.* 馬鈴薯泥
- pumpkin pie [ˋpʌmpkɪn ˏpaɪ] *n.* 南瓜派
- settler [ˋsɛtlə] *n.* 移居者；開拓者
- (the) Pilgrim [ˋpɪlgrɪm] *n.* 1620 年到美國的清教徒
- religious persecution [rɪˋlɪdʒəs ˏpɝsɪˋkjuʃən] *n.* 宗教迫害
- Native American [ˋnetɪv əˋmɛrɪkən] *n.* 美國原住民
- feast [fist] *n.* 盛宴；酒席
- stuffing [ˋstʌfɪŋ] *n.* 餡
- biscuit [ˋbɪskɪt] *n.* 比司吉；餅乾
- breadcrumb [ˋbrɛdˏkrʌmb] *n.* 麵包屑
- spice [spaɪs] *n.* 香料
- bread roll [ˋbrɛd ˏrol] *n.* 麵包捲
- incredible [ɪnˋkrɛdəbl̩] *adj.* 難以置信的；奇妙的

你可以跟我這樣說

CD 2-40

Dialogue B

Annie spends Spring Break at Myrtle Beach, South Carolina.

Liz: Oh man, that was a long car trip.

Annie: At least it only took us six hours instead of nine!

Liz: MapQuest always gives you the slowest possible time. Plus, they calculate the time based on actual speed limits.

Annie: Right. Besides, we saw lots of great scenery.

Liz: No doubt. Hey, there's a parking space. Park there.

Annie: I think we're in apartment 3D. I hope all the beds haven't been taken.

Liz: Well, there are twelve of us sharing an apartment for six. We may have to sleep on the floor ... or crash on the couch.

Annie: Good thing we brought our sleeping bags.

Liz: Come on ... let's dump our stuff in the room and head to the beach!

The girls go to the beach to find their friends.

Annie: Hey, there's Katie. I didn't know she'd be here.

Liz: I think everyone from our school is here. The beach is packed!

Annie: Should we get an umbrella?

Liz: Nah, I want to get some sun. You definitely need a tan. You're too pale!

Annie: What? There's no way I'm getting dark. I bought SPF 50 sunblock.

Liz: Well, I'm going to take a dip in the ocean. Then we can have crab legs, lobster, and clam chowder for dinner!

Annie: OK. I'll keep an eye on our stuff until you get back. Be careful!

安妮到南卡羅來納州的瑪爾托海灘度春假。

莉姿：喔，老天，這趟車程還真久。

安妮：至少只花了我們 6 小時，而不是 9 小時！

莉姿：MapQuest 線上電子地圖計算的都是最慢的車程時間，此外他們還會根據實際的速限計算時間。

安妮：對呀。除此之外，我們還看到了很多漂亮的景色。

莉姿：沒錯。嘿，那裡有個停車位。就停那裡吧。

安妮：我想我們應該是住 3D 公寓。希望還有空床。

莉姿：嗯，我們 12 個人分一間 6 人公寓，有的人可能得睡地上……或者睡沙發了。

安妮：好在我們帶了睡袋。

莉姿：來吧……把東西丟到房間裡，到海邊玩！

兩個女生到海邊找朋友。

安妮：嘿，凱蒂在那邊。我不知道她會來。

莉姿：好像學校所有的人都來了。海邊滿滿的都是人！

安妮：我們是不是該拿把傘？

莉姿：不了，我想曬一點太陽。妳絕對需要曬黑一點，妳太蒼白了！

安妮：什麼？我絕不能曬黑。我買了防曬系數 50 的防曬油。

莉姿：嗯，我要去海裡泡一會兒。然後我們晚餐可以吃蟹腿、龍蝦跟蛤蜊濃湯！

安妮：好。我幫大家看管衣物，等妳們回來。小心點！

[Words & Phrases]

- MapQuest [`mæp‚kwɛst] *n.* 一種線上電子地圖
- speed limit [`spid ‚lɪmɪt] *n.* 速限
- parking space [`pɑrkɪŋ ‚spes] *n.* 停車位
- crash [kræʃ] *v.* （俚）睡覺
- sleeping bag [`slipɪŋ ‚bæg] *n.* 睡袋
- dump [dʌmp] *v.* 丟下；拋下
- packed [pækt] *adj.* 人潮擁擠的

- tan [tæn] *n.* 曬成的棕褐膚色
- pale [pel] *adj.* 蒼白
- SPF (=sun protection factor) 防曬系數
- sunblock [`sʌn‚blɑk] *n.* 防曬油
- take a dip 泡一下
- lobster [`lɑbstɚ] *n.* 龍蝦
- clam chowder [`klæm ‚tʃaʊdɚ] *n.* 蛤蜊濃湯

留學 超實用單字

CD 2-41

Holidays 假日

⭐ surf [sɝf] *v.* **衝浪**

You:　　Are you going to learn how to surf?
Friend:　I want to, but I'm afraid I'll wipe out[1] all the time.

你：　　你要學衝浪嗎？
朋友：　我想，但我怕每次都被波浪打翻。

⭐ wave [wev] *n.* **海浪**

Friend:　Wow. Those are some huge waves.
You:　　At least those surfers[2] look like they're having fun.

朋友：　哇，浪還真大。
你：　　至少那些衝浪的人看起來玩得很開心。

⭐ lifeguard [ˈlaɪfˌgard] *n.* **救生員**

You:　　Where's the lifeguard? I think that girl can't swim back to shore.
Friend:　Don't worry. He's already in the water.

你：　　救生員在哪裡？那個女生好像游不回岸邊。
朋友：　別擔心，救生員已經跳進水裡了。

[**Word List**]

1. wipe out （衝浪時）被波浪翻覆　　　2. surfer [ˈsɝfɚ] *n.* 衝浪者

★ boardwalk [`bord,wɔk] *n.* （海岸邊）木板鋪成的步道

Friend: I love walking down the boardwalk at night.
You:　　Me too. There are so many great restaurants in that area[1].

朋友：　我最喜歡晚上到木板道散步了。
你：　　我也是。那一區有好多很棒的餐廳。

★ pier [pɪr] *n.* 碼頭

You:　　We're going to walk down to the pier. Want to come?
Friend: Sure. I think Peter is fishing down there.

你：　　我們要到碼頭那兒走一走。要不要一起來？
朋友：　好啊。我想彼特正在那邊釣魚。

★ high tide [`haɪ `taɪd] *n.* 滿潮（相反詞為 low tide）

You:　　When is high tide today?
Friend: I think it's going to be at night, around 9 p.m.

你：　　今天什麼時候滿潮？
朋友：　我想是晚上 9 點左右。

[**Word List**]

1. area [`ɛrɪə] *n.* 地區；區域

CD **2-42**

★ banana boat [bə`nænə ˌbot] *n.* 香蕉船

You: Let's go on a banana boat!
Friend: No way! Those things always flip over.¹

你：   我們去坐香蕉船吧！
朋友：   才不要！那種船每次都會翻覆。

★ Easter egg hunt [`istɚ ɛg ˌhʌnt] *n.* 復活節尋蛋遊戲

You: What did you do for Spring Break?
Friend: I went to my aunt's for a big Easter egg hunt. The little kids
          loved it.

你：   你春假要做什麼？
朋友：   我去我阿姨家玩大型的復活節尋蛋遊戲。小朋友都很喜歡這活動呢。

★ homeless shelter [`homlɛs ˌʃɛltɚ] *n.* **無家可歸收容所**

Friend: How about spending Thanksgiving Day with me and my family?
You: Sure. But I won't be able to get there until later because I'm
          volunteering² at the homeless shelter for their Thanksgiving
          meal.

朋友：   跟我和我家人一起過感恩節怎麼樣？
你：   好啊。不過我晚點才能到，因為我自願要去無家可歸收容所幫忙感
          恩節大餐。

[**Word List**]

1. flip over 翻轉

2. volunteer [ˌvɑlən`tɪr] *v.* 自願；自動自發

★ intensive summer course [ɪnˈtɛnsɪv ˈsʌmɚ ˌkors] *n.* 密集暑期課程

Friend: So, are you going back to Taiwan for the summer?

You: Yeah, but not until the end. First I'm going to take an intensive summer course in o-chem.[1]

朋友： 你暑假要回台灣嗎？

你： 要，但可能暑假快結束時才會回去。我要先上有機化學的密集暑期課程。

★ can drive [ˈkæn ˌdaɪv] *n.* 罐頭宣傳活動

You: I noticed there is a big pile of canned foods in the Student Center. What's that all about?

Friend: It's a can drive. If you have any canned food to donate[2], you can take it to the Student Center.

你： 我注意到學生中心有一大堆罐頭食物。那是怎麼一回事？

朋友： 它是種罐頭宣傳活動。如果你有罐頭食物要捐獻的話，你可以把它帶到學生中心去。

[Word List]

1. o-chem（＝organic chemistry）*n.* 有機化學

2. donate [ˈdonet] *v.* 捐贈；捐獻

留學 佈告欄

Thanksgiving Day Menu

I'm thankful for...

Roast Turkey · Mashed Potatoes
Glazed¹ Carrots · Candied² Yams
Biscuits · Cranberry Sauce
Stuffing

****

Pumpkin Pie with Whipped Cream³
Pecan⁴ Pie

[翻 譯]

感恩節菜單

因為有以下食物，我的內心充滿感激……

烤火雞	馬鈴薯泥
糖漿紅蘿蔔	糖漬蕃薯
比司吉	蔓越梅醬

火雞餡

****

鮮奶油南瓜派
山核桃派

[Word List]

1. glazed [glezd] *adj.* 澆了糖漿的

2. candied [ˋkændɪd] *adj.* 糖漬的

3. whipped cream [ˋhwɪpt ˌkrim] *n.* 鮮奶油

4. pecan [pɪˋkæn] *n.* 山核桃

留學 智慧王

Fall Break 秋假

雖然有時秋假又稱 K 書假（給你額外的時間準備期中考），但是大部分的美國學生都把這個假期當作學年中第一個回家的機會。這個假期只有幾天，但期間大部分的大學（尤其是那些位於小市鎮的）都會像鬧空城一般。

Winter Break 寒假

外籍學生通常會在寒假時第一次回家。寒假約持續一個月，介於秋季和春季兩學期間。如果你不打算回家，可以把握機會在美國國內旅遊，嘗試新活動，例如滑雪板。

Spring Break 春假

冬天就要結束了，而你也剛考完期中考。春季學期最棒的時段已經到來——春假！春假實際上是落在三月初或三月中，天氣雖仍冷颼颼，但許多學生都會利用這個假期和朋友去海邊玩。瑪爾托海灘、希爾頓頭島和戴托納灘都是很受歡迎的地點。不過也有很多學生會前往牙買加、坎昆和巴哈馬群島。春假被稱為「狂野週」，派對、日光浴和狂飲不可少。盡興的玩、注意安全，並曬些太陽吧！

Summer Vacation 暑假

暑假大約為期三到四個月，是一年當中最長的假期。外籍學生幾乎都會趁這段時間返家。你也可以選擇修一些暑期課程，不過通常沒有絕對必要。所有的外籍學生都有一年「選擇性實習」（OPT）的機會，可以在美國合法工作一年。你可以把實習時間分散在每年暑假，或者在畢業後實習一整年。

Beach Week 海灘週

　　春季學期期末考到畢業典禮之間那一個禮拜，就稱做海灘週。猜得出來為什麼嗎？許多學生會到海邊玩，慶祝學年的結束。每個學校都有他們最喜歡的海灘，所以你可能會感覺好像整個學校突然間都搬到了海邊一個禮拜。海灘週就像春假一樣，充滿了歡慶、飲酒和派對等活動。

Beach Vocab 海灘相關詞彙

Swimsuits 泳裝　　　　　　　　　　　　　　　　　　　CD **2-43**

- **1-piece** [`wʌn ˌpis] 　　　　　　　　　*n.* 連身泳裝
- **tankini** [tænˋkinɪ] 　　　　　　　　　*n.* 小可愛比基尼
- **swim trunks** [`swim ˌtrʌŋks] 　　　　　*n.* 泳褲

Seafood 海鮮　　　　　　　　　　　　　　　　　　　　CD **2-44**

- **shrimp** [ʃrɪmp] 　　　　　　　　　　　*n.*（小）蝦
- **prawn** [prɔn] 　　　　　　　　　　　　*n.* 明蝦；大蝦
- **crawfish** [`krɔˌfiʃ] 　　　　　　　　　*n.* 小龍蝦
- **oyster** [`ɔɪstɚ] 　　　　　　　　　　　*n.* 生蠔；牡蠣
- **mussel** [`mʌsḷ] 　　　　　　　　　　　*n.* 貽貝；淡菜
- **clam** [klæm] 　　　　　　　　　　　　*n.* 蛤蜊
- **tuna** [`tunə] 　　　　　　　　　　　　*n.* 鮪魚
- **salmon** [`sæmən] 　　　　　　　　　　*n.* 鮭魚
- **cod** [kɑd] 　　　　　　　　　　　　　*n.* 鱈魚

Did You Know...? 你知道嗎……？

　　很多美國學生都有兼職工作，尤其是在暑假期間。較普遍的工作包括了在咖啡廳、餐廳或服飾店打工，但也有的會選擇在寒假或暑假時做實習（intern-ship）。實習就是不給薪的寒、暑期工作（雖然有時會給一點補助），因此學生在公司或機構工作時可以獲得實務上的經驗。另一個選擇是在春假時做外部實習（externship）。外部實習是極短暫的密集實習訓練，為期僅一個禮拜。你有機會接觸實務，但不須承擔太大的義務。如果不確定未來要做什麼，並希望預先瞭解某個工作，這是很不錯的選擇。

國家圖書館出版品預行編目資料

留學英文很有聊 / Lily Yang 作；金振寧譯.
——初版.——臺北市；貝塔，2005〔民94〕
　　面；　　公分

　ISBN 957-729-524-X（平裝附光碟片）

　1. 英國語言—會話

805.188　　　　　　　　　　　94011782

留學英文很有聊

Conversation Boosters — Campus Life

作　　者 / Lily Yang（楊智媛）
總 編 審 / 王復國
譯　　者 / 金振寧
執行編輯 / 廖姿菱

出　　版 / 貝塔出版有限公司
地　　址 / 台北市 100 館前路 12 號 11 樓
電　　話 / (02)2314-2525
傳　　真 / (02)2312-3535
郵　　撥 / 19493777 貝塔出版有限公司
客服專線 / (02)2314-3535
客服信箱 / btservice@betamedia.com.tw

總 經 銷 / 時報文化出版企業股份有限公司
地　　址 / 桃園縣龜山鄉萬壽路二段 351 號　　　　　樓
電　　話 / (02) 2306-6842

出版日期 / 2005 年 8 月初版一刷
定　　價 / 299 元
ISBN：957-729-524-X

喚醒你的英文語感 ！

對折後釘好，直接寄回即可！

| 廣　告　回　信 |
| 北區郵政管理局登記證 |
| 北 台 字 第 1 4 2 5 6 號 |
| 免　貼　郵　票 |

100 台北市中正區館前路12號11樓

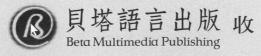 收

 寄件者住址 □□□

貝塔語言出版
Beta Multimedia Publishing

讀者服務專線（02）2314-3535　　讀者服務傳真（02）2312-353
客戶服務信箱 btservice@betamedia.com.tw

www.betamedia.com.tw

謝謝您購買本書！！

貝塔語言擁有最優良之英文學習書籍，為提供您最佳的英語學習資訊，您可填妥此表後寄回（免貼郵票）將可不定期收到本公司最新發行書訊及活動訊息！

姓名：＿＿＿＿＿＿＿＿＿＿＿　性別：□男 □女　生日：＿＿＿年＿＿＿月＿＿＿日

電話：(公)＿＿＿＿＿＿＿＿＿(宅)＿＿＿＿＿＿＿＿＿(手機)＿＿＿＿＿＿＿＿

電子信箱：＿＿＿＿＿＿＿＿＿＿＿＿＿＿＿＿＿＿＿＿＿＿＿

學歷：□高中職含以下　□專科　□大學　□研究所含以上

職業：□金融　□服務　□傳播　□製造　□資訊　□軍公教　□出版

　　　□自由　□教育　□學生　□其他

職級：□企業負責人　□高階主管　□中階主管　□職員　□專業人士

1. 您購買的書籍是？＿＿＿＿＿＿＿＿＿＿＿＿＿＿＿＿＿

2. 您從何處得知本產品？(可複選)

　　　□書店 □網路 □書展 □校園活動 □廣告信函 □他人推薦 □新聞報導 □其他

3. 您覺得本產品價格：

　　　□偏高 □合理 □偏低

4. 請問目前您每週花了多少時間學英語？

　　　□ 不到十分鐘 □ 十分鐘以上，但不到半小時 □ 半小時以上，但不到一小時

　　　□ 一小時以上，但不到兩小時 □ 兩個小時以上 □ 不一定

5. 通常在選擇語言學習書時，哪些因素是您會考慮的？

　　　□ 封面 □ 內容、實用性 □ 品牌 □ 媒體、朋友推薦 □ 價格 □ 其他＿＿＿＿＿

6. 市面上您最需要的語言書種類為？

　　　□ 聽力 □ 閱讀 □ 文法 □ 口說 □ 寫作 □ 其他＿＿＿＿＿＿

7. 通常您會透過何種方式選購語言學習書籍？

　　　□ 書店門市 □ 網路書店 □ 郵購 □ 直接找出版社 □ 學校或公司團購

　　　□ 其他＿＿＿＿＿＿＿

8. 給我們的建議：＿＿＿＿＿＿＿＿＿＿＿＿＿＿＿＿＿＿＿＿＿＿

＿＿＿＿＿＿＿＿＿＿＿＿＿＿＿＿＿＿＿＿＿＿＿＿＿＿＿＿＿

喚醒你的英文語感 !

Get a Feel for English !

喚醒你的英文語感！

Get a Feel for English !